Large Print Lynde
**Saving Miss Julie
/ Stan Lynde.**

Oct 2007

SAVING MISS JULIE

**Center Point
Large Print**

**This Large Print Book carries the
Seal of Approval of N.A.V.H.**

SAVING MISS JULIE

Stan Lynde

CENTER POINT PUBLISHING
THORNDIKE, MAINE

This Center Point Large Print edition
is published in the year 2007 by arrangement with
Cottonwood Publishing.

Cover art by Stan Lynde.

The text of this Large Print edition is unabridged. In other
aspects, this book may vary from the original edition. Printed in
Thailand. Set in 16-point Times New Roman type.

ISBN-10: 1-60285-021-6
ISBN-13: 978-1-60285-021-7

Library of Congress Cataloging-in-Publication Data

Lynde, Stan, 1931-
    Saving Miss Julie / Stan Lynde.--Center Point large print ed.
        p. cm.
    ISBN-13: 978-1-60285-021-7 (lib. bdg. : alk. paper)
    1. Kidnapping--Fiction. 2. Montana--Fiction. 3. Large type books. I. Title.

PS3562.Y439S28 2007
813'.54--dc22

2007006095

To my daughter
Shannon

and to granddaughters
Amy Lynn, Michelle, Kelsey,
Chelsea, Cortney, Trisha,
Amanda, Kaitlin, and
Eleanor Scout

None of whom, and all of whom,
are like Julie

SAVING MISS JULIE

one

I was playing cribbage with Glenn Murdoch, the undersheriff, when Boogles McFee stomped into the marshal's office and bawled that he'd been robbed.

"It was that shifty-eyed kid I hired as swamper," Boogles said. "Damn sneak took sixteen dollars and forty-two cents from the till and absconded his butt to parts unknown."

Boogles had come in a hurry. He still wore his bartender's apron, and I noticed his brogans had tracked a good five pounds of spring mud in off the street. His face was flushed dull red going to purple; a betting man would have put his money on a heart attack. Glenn laid his cards down and fixed Boogles with a reproachful gaze. "Damn, Boogles," he said. "I just cleaned that floor."

"Well, excuse me all to hell," Boogles huffed, "but a robbery has took place here in Dry Creek, and I thought you jist might like to know about it."

Glenn slid his chair back and stood up. He gave me a lopsided grin and a wink. "You're right, Boogles," he said. "When did this here crime of the century take place?"

"Not half an hour ago," said Boogles. "I left that fool Delbert Snodgrass to mind the bar while I went out to the hooter. When I came back he was gone and so was my damn money."

Glenn stuck his hands in his back pockets and looked out the window. Overhead, big-bellied clouds, purple as plums, scowled above the valley. Rain was falling again, as it had almost daily since the middle of June. The rutted street outside was a soupy blend of muck, mire, and dirty water.

"How did the kid make his getaway?" Glenn asked. "He still ridin' that glass-eyed Indian pony?"

"I guess. Pony's gone, too. Was tied out front when I left the Oasis, gone when I came back."

Glenn looked thoughtful. He turned away from the window and sat down again across from me. "I'll have Delbert and your money back here inside the hour," he told Boogles. "Now go on back to work before some other desperado makes off with your watered whiskey."

Boogles jaw dropped. He frowned. Twice he started to say something but failed to get the words out. Finally, he turned on his heel and marched out into the rain.

"Deal the cards, Merlin," said Glenn. "We've got time aplenty to finish our game."

I had knowed Glenn Murdoch for the better part of my twenty-one years, and I admired him. Growing up on my folks' place south of Dry Creek, I had come to know most of the cowpunchers in that part of the country. Glenn had been one of the best until his night horse fell on him during a cattle run and left him with a stiff leg and a full-time limp.

Later, when Ernie Fillmore had bought enough drinks and kissed enough babies to get himself elected county sheriff, he'd hired Glenn as his under-sheriff. Like I said, Glenn had been a top cowhand, and it wasn't long until he was a top lawman as well. To my way of thinking he'd have made a better sheriff than Ernie Fillmore, but then I'd had a run-in or two with Ernie so it could be I was prejudiced.

Glenn was a better than average hand with a revolver and he could hold his own in anything from a rough-and-tumble to a riot, but the quality I admired most about him was the way he used his head.

Take this day I'm talking about, for example. When Boogles reported the robbery, Glenn didn't light out directly in pursuit of the fugitive. He took a look at the weather, considered the situation, and went back to our cribbage game. And all the while, Delbert Snodgrass, sometime swamper from the Oasis Saloon, was riding out across the gumbo, free as a bird and with a brain to match.

Glenn caught a double run the next hand, made a second pair on the cut, and counted twenty-four points to win the game. "That's three in a row you've lost, Merlin," he said. "Maybe you'll be lucky in love."

"I've got no complaints," I told him. "My bad luck seems to happen mostly when I play cribbage with you. Anyway, that last game was fairly close 'til you skunked me."

Glenn pulled open his desk drawer and put the

cards and board away. He looked thoughtful, stroking his jaw with his thumb as he watched the rain rattle against the window. "Tell me if I'm wrong," he said, "but you ain't been gainfully employed since you wrangled broncs for the M Cross this spring, have you?"

"You know I ain't. Mostly, I've caught up on my sleep, healed some of my horse-inflicted wounds, and waited for the Lord to either run out of rain or send down plans for buildin' an ark. Why do you ask?"

"It just occurred to me that if you ain't workin' that could make you a vagrant. And vagrancy is against the law."

"I ain't no vagrant. I'm retired."

"The thing is, Merlin, somebody has to go bring Delbert back. Ordinarily, that would be me, seein' as I draw pay as undersheriff. But with all this wet weather my bad leg is botherin' me a good deal more than somewhat. How'd you like to go collect him for me?"

"So then I'd be employed and a vagrant no more, huh? Nice try, Glenn, but like you said, you wear the badge, I don't."

"Got a box full of badges. I can make you a special deputy."

Well, hell. Like I said, I admired Glenn. I knowed his leg hurt him bad sometimes. Besides, rain or no rain, the idea of chasing down a runaway thief sort of tickled my fancy. "What does this special deputy job pay?" I asked.

12

"Supper at Ignacio's tonight, on me," Glenn said, grinning.

I raised my right hand and throwed out my chest. "All right," I said, "evildoers beware! Merlin Fanshaw, manhunter, is a-comin'."

Glenn swore me in. As I recall, the oath bound me to uphold the laws of Montana Territory and do whatever Glenn told me to, 'til death do us part. He pinned a badge onto my shirt and gave me a snort of whiskey from a bottle he kept on hand in case of snake bite, rainy weather, or whatever.

"I figure you'll catch up with Delbert somewhere this side of the river," Glenn said. "I expect he'll already be tired of the wild, free outlaw life. He might even be glad to see you.

"But don't take your own horse," Glenn said. "Instead, go down to the livery and put a saddle on Big Mildred, my mule. She's what you need to get this job done."

Now Big Mildred was a local celebrity around Dry Creek. Born of a Belgian mare and a mammoth jack, she stood a good seventeen hands high and was strong as a locomotive. She was sort of a pet of Glenn's, and while she wasn't likely to win any beauty contests, the old girl had a sweet nature and a willing spirit. I was about to ask Glenn why I should ride his mule on my muddy manhunt when he told me.

"The muck out there is hub deep to a water wheel," he said. "I figure Delbert's pony has gave out on him by now and left him afoot. That would mean our sneak thief is likely pretty well played out himself. Shouldn't take much of a tracker to follow his trail."

I took my slicker down from the peg by the door, slipped it on, and stepped outside. Glenn stood watching from the doorway as I high-heeled my way up the rain-slick boardwalk toward the livery stable. Five minutes later I had caught and saddled Big Mildred and was riding her out of town.

Most mules have short, thick heads and small, narrow hoofs, but Big Mildred must have took after her mama. Mildred had a long, sorrowful face whose features included a big Roman nose at one end, and a huge pair of long, hairy ears on the other. Her feet were less than dainty. Fact is, they could each have well-nigh covered a dinner plate. But Glenn was right. Old Mildred turned out to be just what the doctor ordered.

Now if you've never spent springtime on the northern plains you might not be familiar with gumbo mud. We don't generally get much rain up here, but when we do it can turn the soil to a gummy goo that'd make your everyday quagmire seem like a dance floor. Wet gumbo bogs down cattle, mucks up wagon wheels, and plum restricts the progress of whatever tries to travel upon it. I believe that under the right circumstances gumbo mud could swaller a freight train, tracks and all. Anyway, such was the murky muck Mildred and me—and Delbert, the runaway thief—were dealing with that morning.

14

As Glenn had surmised, Delbert wasn't hard to track. His trail led southwest, his pony's hoofprints plain as bullet holes in a bathtub. Delbert had lit out at a full gallop to begin with, the feet of his glass-eyed steed gouging great holes in the wet earth and flinging gobs of sod far out behind.

Before long, I could see where his mount had slowed to a trot, then to a walk. I knowed my hunt was nearing its end.

Sure enough, maybe a mile farther on at the edge of a long coulee I came upon the pony. The animal stood, bogged down and spent, too tired even to take my notice. Delbert's footprints led away up the draw toward a sagebrush-studded ridge. Twice I found places where he'd stopped and tried to scrape the mud off his boots. Plain on the hillside, I saw where he'd fallen and struggled to his feet again. Pulling my six-shooter, I checked its loads and turned Old Mildred back around the face of the slope.

Not twenty feet from the top of the ridge, looking more like a drowned rat than a desperado, Delbert sat hugging himself and shivering in the wet grass. His feet and legs were caked with mud halfway to his knees; it looked like each foot would weigh thirty pounds or better. Soaked by the downpour, his hat brim drooped down over his face and neck like pie dough. Delbert had no idea I was there until I was upon him. When he seen Mildred's big feet stop in front of him he jerked his hat off and jumped up, but I had the drop on him and he knew it.

15

"You're under arrest, pardner," I told him. "I'm takin' you back to town."

Delbert's shoulders slumped. Bloodhound sad, his eyes looked up at me. His lower lip quivered. For a moment I thought he was going to cry.

"Oh, thank you, Merlin," he choked.

I took the stolen money and a rusty old Starr revolver off Delbert. His woebegone Indian pony looked to be plumb tuckered out, so I resolved to leave the animal and fetch it back to town later. Delbert and me then struck out for Dry Creek, holding to the high ground. Of course, I could have stayed in the saddle and made Delbert walk ahead of me, but he looked so pitiful I wound up leading Mildred and walking at his side. It was less boggy on the ridges, but the mud still clung with every step like oatmeal cooked too long.

"Damn, Delbert," I said. "What was you thinking of? It don't hardly seem like sixteen dollars and forty-two cents was worth all this trouble."

"Well, hell, Merlin," Delbert sulled, "I never claimed to be no Jesse James."

"I know, but if you was going to turn outlaw it does seem you might have robbed something more profitable than Boogles' till."

"Like what?"

"Well, like the bank, maybe. That's where the money is."

Delbert raised up his floppy hat brim and fixed me with a scornful stare. "The *bank?* Can you see me

16

tryin' to hold up the damn *bank?* That snotty little bank teller would have laughed 'til he peed himself. No, I just needed some travelin' money to get shut of Boogles' meanness and go on to a new job."

I almost felt sorry for him, but I figured he should have knowed better. "Well," I said, "you know what they say—crime don't pay."

Delbert stuck his hands in his pockets and stared at the soggy ground. "It sure don't pay *much*," he agreed.

Glenn was waiting under the board awning in front of the marshal's office when I brought Delbert in. Carefully, Glenn looked the kid up and down, from his muddy boots to his soggy hat. Then he slowly shook his head from side to side, as if he was seeing some rare specimen in a zoo. "No offense, son," he told Delbert, "but I'm not letting you in my jail until you clean up some." Glenn turned to me. "Take the prisoner around back to the pump and wash off some of that gumbo. Then bring him in the back way."

I unpinned the badge from my shirt. "I signed on to fetch him back, not wash him," I said.

"That supper I'm buyin' tonight includes fresh apple pie."

"All right," I said, putting the badge back on, "but I draw the line at tuckin' him in and readin' him a bedtime story."

Meek as a lamb and naked as truth, Delbert hunkered under the pump spout while I worked the handle. When I'd cleaned him up as well as I could, Glenn gave him a blanket to wrap himself in and set him by the woodstove to dry. Delbert was shivering like a wet dog, and his teeth were chattering, but he looked some better, anyway. I gave Glenn the stolen money and the kid's revolver and made ready to go. "I'll take Old Mildred to the livery," I told Glenn, "and fetch Delbert's horse back. I'll see you at Ignacio's around six."

"I'm obliged, Merlin," Glenn said. "See you then."

Just before I walked out the door, I said my goodbys to Delbert. "Just curious," I said, "but that job you mentioned—was there someplace special you were headed?"

"Lander, Wyoming," he said. "When Billy Christmas stopped by the Oasis this spring, he told me I should come see him there if I was ever down that way. You remember Billy Christmas, don't you, Merlin?"

"Oh, yes," I said. "I remember Billy Christmas."

Now before I tell you about Billy Christmas and what he has to do with anything, I need to step off the trail a pace or two and tell you about Thane McAllister and his daughter Julie.

Thane McAllister was the biggest cowman in our part of the country, and his M Cross ranch took in the better part of Progress County. When I say McAllister was a big cowman, I mean that his range covered a heap of territory and he had more cattle than God. But

Thane was big in other ways, too. He had a big bank account, big ambitions, and a heart the size of a buffalo's. Thane was big-bodied, too. He weighed right at three hundred pounds, and when he walked around, the earth shook. He sat a big saddle, of course, which meant any horse he rode had to carry pritnear three hundred and fifty pounds. His personal mounts were big, blocky horses that tipped the scales at better than 1,250 pounds each. They tended to be slow starters, but they were hell for stout.

Raising beef was good business in that year of 1885. A man could buy a steer for $5, sell it for between $45 and $60, and run his entire operation on free government grass. There were losses, of course—wolves, rustlers, and winter-kill took their toll—but there was real money in cattle, especially for the big operators. Like I said, Thane McAllister was one of the biggest.

Now you would think that with all his money Thane would be a happy man, but that's not how it was. My pa used to say money can't buy happiness but it can rent it sometimes. I wouldn't know if that's true, not ever having had enough cash to make a proper test, but I do know Thane McAllister had misery aplenty even if he was a cattle baron.

Consumption had took his wife Lucinda six years before, and her dying like to broke Thane's big heart altogether. He went away somewheres inside himself and throwed up a wall nobody could get through. That wouldn't have been so bad, maybe, except his only daughter Julie couldn't get through either.

Julie McAllister was only twelve at the time, but it seemed like she took her mother's passing even harder than Thane did. What she needed was for her daddy to put his arms around her and tell her everything was going to be all right, but Thane never done that. I guess he didn't know how. Thane knowed about the range and cowpunchers and what the mama cow said to her calf, but he didn't know straight up about a young girl's needs. I reckon he loved her all right, he just didn't know how to show it. So he sent Julie off to a boarding school back east and hoped for the best. The best ain't what he got.

The first few years, everything seemed to go pretty well. Julie stayed at the school nine months of the year and spent her summers back at the ranch. I used to see her sometimes in Dry Creek with her dad, but there always seemed to be an air of sadness about her. I asked her how she was once, and she told me she was happy. It's not for me to say she wasn't, but happy was not the first thing that came to mind when a person saw her.

It wasn't long before the rumors drifted back home. Julie and another girl had got into some blackberry brandy somewheres and had to be brought back to school by the police. Julie was sneaking off and spending her days riding horses in the city park. Julie was keeping company with a stable boy and staying out past the school's curfew. It was all just gossip, you know, but it did seem that everything was not well back there at Miss Chatelaine's School for Young Ladies.

Thane paid a few visits to the school—to smooth Miss Chatelaine's ruffled feathers and try to straighten Julie out, people said. Then a year ago, after his third trip east in as many months, Thane throwed in the towel and brought Julie home to stay.

I had signed on with the M Cross that spring as horse wrangler for the roundup, and it was early May when I rode out to the home ranch. Like other big outfits, the M Cross generally took on a bronc stomper to work the rough string, but the man they'd hired hadn't showed up yet. I told Waco Calhoun, Thane's foreman, that I wanted to handle my own horses. He allowed that I could. There was six head in my string, and I commenced working them by day down at the round corral. I took my meals over at the cook shack and spent my nights rubbing linament on my sore places.

The M Cross had the reputation of providing good horses to their cowhands, and the six ponies they gave me seemed honest and willing. They all bucked some at first saddle, of course. They'd been running free all winter and were full of new grass and feeling frisky. I suppose they were curious about me as well and did their buck-jumping to see what kind of rider they'd got theirselves assigned to. I trimmed their manes and tails and worked all six in the round corral until I was satisfied they'd be reliable under saddle.

Well, about the time I thought I had my work pretty well finished, the big, sleepy-eyed sorrel in my string swallowed his head one morning and took me to church. I had been working on his reining—turning him double, stopping, and whatnot—and I had figured to give him a lesson in backing up. Apparently, this skill was not in the sorrel's repertoire, and he had no real desire to learn it. He boiled over and went to chinning the moon, and he nearly unloaded me the first jump.

He had took me by surprise and no mistake. I lost my right stirrup, found it again, and bounced all over the saddle until I got myself centered and began to make a ride. I commenced to punish the big horse with my spurs, and I stuck to him like stink to a skunk. Directly his pitching began to slow, but I took a deep seat and kept on a-spurring until at length he hollered uncle and went back to behaving himself.

It had been a near thing, but it had ended well. I hadn't been throwed, the big sorrel's tantrum had been dealt with, and he had repented of his folly.

I rode him around the corral, then turned and rode him back the other way. I reined him to the left and to the right. I even backed him up without protest on his part. Finally, I stepped down and rubbed his neck, talking to him soft and telling him what a blue ribbon cowhorse he was.

I had been so busy dealing with the sorrel's rebellion that I hadn't saw the rider draw rein. "I see they put old Rusty in your string," said a soft voice. "That was quite a ride you made."

I jerked my head around so fast I'm surprised I didn't break my neck. There, just outside the corral, sat Julie McAllister astride a handsome black mare. I hadn't seen her since she'd come back to the ranch. I recalled her as a big-eyed freckle-faced kid, long of limb, and awkward as a new foal. One look told me my recollection was seriously out of date. Julie had changed so much that I scarcely recognized her. She had filled out in all the right places and had growed to be a fine-looking woman. Her eyes were still big, and they were dark and deep now in the fading light of late afternoon. Beneath a pearl gray Stetson, her long hair cascaded down her back, black as her eyes, black as the mare she rode. There was nothing of the awkward youngster about her any longer. Julie sat her silver-mounted saddle with confidence and grace. Only her smile seemed the same, sweet and clean, but shadowed by sorrow.

"Uh—howdy, Julie—uh, Miss McAllister," I stammered, snatching my hat off. "I reckon the red son of a—the sorrel—caught me off guard."

She laughed. "No need to apologize," she said. "You really made a fine ride. And you can call me Julie. I haven't changed all that much, have I?"

"Uh—no, ma'am. I mean yes, ma'am. You're looking fine, Miss, uh—Julie."

"Thanks, Merlin. Waco tells me you're going out with the roundup this year."

23

"Yes'm. I'm jingler for the outfit—the horse wrangler."

The sun set as we spoke, and the shadows growed long. Up at the main house, lamplight glowed yellow in the windows. Julie glanced toward the house, then back at me. "I expect I'd better let you go," she said. "It'll be supper time soon. Good to see you again, Merlin."

She smiled her sad smile, turned the mare away, and rode off toward the horse barn. I watched her ride away until I lost her in the twilight.

two

I spent the next few mornings working the horses in my string and putting the finishing touches to their education. All six of them had settled down and seemed ready to work, even the sorrel Julie had called "Rusty." I was looking forward to the roundup. The rough string rider still hadn't showed up. Except for the chore boy and a couple of old-timers I pretty much had the bunkhouse to myself.

I hadn't seen Julie to talk to since that day at the corral, but that doesn't mean she wasn't in my thoughts. I found myself remembering her sweet, sad smile and the way her eyes captured and held mine. I recalled how her black hair shone in the sunlight and the way my name sounded when she said it. Julie was the last thing I thought about before drifting off to sleep and the first thing every morning. I began each day with the hope that I'd see her again, and I nearly had more than one serious horse wreck because my mind was on Julie instead of the broncs.

I did see her once from a distance. She was riding the hills above the ranch on her black mare, sunlight glinting off the silver conchos of her saddle. Julie sat a horse well, her back straight and her feet well forward in the stirrups, and she made a mighty pretty picture in the late afternoon light.

Along about week's end Waco and me gathered the horses from their winter range and brought them in to the big corrals at the ranch. While I manned the gate, Waco cut out the rank and salty stock that made up the rough string. "I expect that bronc stomper any day now," Waco said. "He's supposed to be good, and he'd sure as hell better be. Some of these old rips eat bronc twisters for breakfast."

Two days later, just before chuck, I was out in front of the bunkhouse waiting for the dinner bell when I saw a horseman coming up the road. He looked to be about my age and size, and he set his saddle as though he'd been born to it. His saddlehorse was a blaze-faced gray, and he carried his bedroll atop a bay pack-horse behind him. As I watched, the rider swung on up the road, clattered over the bridge across Little Otter Creek, and came straight toward the bunkhouse. I stood up, watching him come on, and nodded as he drew rein.

The gent smiled, his teeth even and white against the darkness of his skin, and his gray eyes smiled, too. "Howdy," he said, "I'm Billy Christmas. I'm here to ride this outfit's rough string. Know where I can find Waco Calhoun?"

I reached my hand up, and he bent low in the saddle to take it.

"Merlin Fanshaw," I said. "Horse wrangler. Calhoun's been expecting you. Throw your roll on a bunk inside and I'll help you put your horses up."

The rider stepped down and gave me his honest smile again. "Much obliged," he said. "That's neighborly of you."

"Glad to do it," says I, and I was.

I guess you could say Billy Christmas and me hit it off right from the start. We got to know each other well over the next few weeks, and the better I knowed him the more I liked him. He was a year older than me, easy-going and good-natured, and if he didn't talk much I guess I more than made up for that.

He did tell me he had growed up on his daddy's horse ranch near Lander, Wyoming, and that his mother was a full-blood Shoshone woman. Like mine, his daddy had passed away some years previous, and I could tell Billy still missed him.

He used to talk about that Wyoming ranch like it was the best part of paradise. He would describe the creek that ran through the place, the way the hills lay, and how the house and barns were set up until I almost felt I had been there. He said he took work as a bronc rider to help pay for the place, and that it would all be his one day.

Billy was dark of skin, with hair the blue-black hue of a raven's wing, and I figured he got his coloring from his ma.

There were thirteen mighty tough horses in the rough string, including a few snaky old hammer-heads, three or four green-broke mustangs, and a couple of genuine man-haters. They was hard to get on and harder to stay on, but Billy just took them in his stride like it was all in a day's work, which for him I guess it was.

My pa and me used to go mustanging when I was a kid. We broke wild horses to ride, after which Pa would sell them to the cow outfits over along the Big Porcupine. I had knowed some fine bronc stompers in those days and one or two good ones since, but it didn't take me long to decide that Billy Christmas was among the very best I'd seen.

Some riders abuse horses and break them down by harsh treatment. Some handle every horse the same, as if the animals were stamped out of metal by a blacksmith. I suppose those fellers don't know any better, or maybe they're in a hurry to get the work done and draw their pay. Whatever the reason, those men don't generally hold their jobs for long. That kind of treatment spoils a horse, and no decent cow outfit will put up with it.

The truth is, every horse is different. Some learn

quick, and some never do. Some have been mistreated and fight back out of fear. Some are stubborn
and willful. And a few horses just go hog-wild and
snake crazy for no apparent reason. A good rough
string rider gets to know his animals and handles each
one according to its need. That's how Billy Christmas
did the job. I never saw him lose his temper, and he
treated his string with kindness.

Of course, there's kindness and then there's kindness. Sometimes a horse needs a rider who will get
above him and sap him out to where he changes his
attitude. That was the case with a big gelding from
Billy's string the boys called Hoodlum. Hoodlum
tipped the scales at 1,200 pounds, and most of it was
high explosive. He'd had a lot of luck at bucking his
riders off, and he'd hurt a few of them pretty bad.

I was watching Billy roping broncs in the round
corral one afternoon when Hoodlum made a run at
him, biting and striking with his front feet, chock full
of hate and harboring murder in his heart. Billy just
stepped aside, dabbed a loop over those slashing front
feet, and dumped Hoodlum on his ear. Before the
bronc could get up again, Billy tied all four of his feet
together in a bunch. Then he walked off and left the
old renegade to ponder his wicked ways.

There was a good spring in a little patch of cat-tails
just below the main house, and Billy and me went up
there and had us a drink of cold water. Billy rolled
himself a smoke and we sat in the shade and talked
for awhile. When we'd been there maybe thirty min-

utes, Billy stood up and squinted at the sun. "Time to get back to work," he said, and we headed back down to the horse corral.

After he'd picked up his saddle and hackamore, Billy went inside the corral and untied Hoodlum. Before the bronc could decide what to do next, Billy slipped the hackamore and saddle on him. Then Billy swung up onto the horse's back in one smooth motion. That's when old Hoodlum came unglued. He blew up like a black-powder bomb, squealing and bellering and popping his backbone, while Billy matched the horse move for move and made it look easy.

The big horse twisted and pitched, spun and dodged. He jumped straight up and came down like a dropped boulder. He swapped ends, spun like a whirligig, and throwed his belly at the sky. And when he'd finally played all the cards in his deck, he stood still, dripping wet and quivering, his sides heaving and his breath coming in racking gasps.

Billy kicked him into a run and took the horse clockwise around the corral. He reversed him and rode him back the other way. He drew rein and stepped down. Then he stood close beside the panting animal and stroked its neck, speaking low. "There's no call for you to fight me, big horse," he said. "I'll treat you as well as you'll allow. Nothing to fear. All is well." Then Billy stripped off the saddle and hackamore, opened the corral gate, and turned Hoodlum out with the rest of the string.

29

That's when I noticed Julie. As she had that time with me, Julie McAllister had quietly approached the corral to watch the action. She had climbed to the top rail and sat there, one gloved hand on the upright and the other on the rail beside her. Her pearl gray Stetson shaded her face and caused her dark eyes to seem darker still. Beneath a tight-fitting vest of black wool, Julie wore a white shirt with bloused sleeves. A red silk scarf was loosely knotted at her throat, and hand-made boots with silver spurs showed below the fringe of her riding skirt. She was altogether as pretty as a sunrise.

It took me a second or two, but I finally remembered my manners and snatched my hat off. I was about to tell her I was glad to see her when I saw she wasn't looking at me. She sat perfectly still on that top rail, her lips slightly parted and her dark eyes fixed on Billy.

Billy stood straight up, his saddle in one hand and the hackamore in the other, and stared at Julie as though he was seeing a vision. I swear I felt electricity dry and hot in the air like those times in summer when a lightning storm moves through. Julie seemed drawn to Billy like steel dust to a magnet. As for Billy, well, he looked at Julie exactly the way a cat looks at cream.

"Howdy, Julie," I said, "I didn't see you come up." She smiled, but her eyes never left Billy. "This is Billy Christmas, the rough string rider," I told her. "Billy, meet Miss Julie, Thane's daughter."

Billy came out of his trance. Still looking at Julie, he slowly lowered the saddle and took off his hat. "I'm very pleased to meet you, Miss Julie," he said, as if that wasn't already plenty obvious.

"Thank you," said Julie, "I must say you seem to know your way around horses. I like to watch a bronc rider who knows his trade."

"It's a rough trade, Miss, but yes, it's the one I know."

They both fell silent then, but their eyes kept up the conversation.

Neither Julie nor Billy paid me any more mind than if I was a horse apple in the dust. They didn't seem to know I was even there. The way they kept gazing at one another put me in mind of that schoolyard game where kids lock eyes, and the first one who blinks loses. I reckon neither of them would have noticed if a tornado had blowed through the corral.

I don't know how long the staring contest would have went on if something hadn't come along to break it up, but the fact is something, or rather someone, did. Just outside the corral stood the bull of the woods himself, Julie's daddy and our boss, Thane McAllister. Thane stood solid as a tree, his boots planted wide in the loose dirt. Beneath a white walrus moustache, his chin jutted forward like a granite ledge. He squinted up at his daughter. "Get down off of there, Julie," he said quietly. "These boys have work to do."

Thane opened the gate and stepped inside. "You'd be Bill Christmas," he said, sizing Billy up. "I'm told you're a top hand when it comes to setting the wild and the snuffy ones."

"That's what you're paying me for," Billy said, smiling.

Thane's eyes widened, then narrowed again. Close up, he seemed even bigger than his three hundred pounds. "Why, yes," he said, smiling, "that, and *only* that."

Julie hadn't come down from the top rail as Thane had told her to. Below her hat brim her brows met in the beginnings of a frown, and her jaw took on a stubborn set. Thane spoke to her again, and there was just the hint of an edge to his voice. "I'd like you to walk up to the house with me, sweetheart," he said, and Julie reluctantly stepped down from her perch. Her black mare stood just outside the corral where she'd left it, and Thane nodded at the animal, then turned to me. "Put my daughter's mare up, will you, Merlin? I don't expect Julie will be needing her again today."

"Sure," I said. "Be glad to."

" 'Obliged," he said. "See you boys."

I stepped around behind the corral and took hold of the mare's reins. Thane held Julie's elbow as they walked away together, and he seemed to be talking to her with considerable feeling. Of course, I couldn't hear what he was saying, but whatever it was Julie didn't seem to be making any reply. She just walked on with a stubborn set to her shoulders and her head held high. I couldn't help noticing, though, that just as they turned up the path to the house, Julie took a last quick look back over her shoulder at Billy.

During the next week Doughbelly Pierce, the roundup cook, began readying the wagons, checking the tents and tarps for rips and holes, and making such other repairs as were needed. Four more cow-punchers showed up at the ranch and rolled out their beds in the bunkhouse. Most of the boys had worked together before, so there was considerable joshing and tale-telling concerning times remembered. Waco picked out the horses for each rider's string, and I practiced some in the corral at roping them for the boys.

Most nights there was a poker game in the bunkhouse. Using matches as chips, the boys would play against their future earnings, and I generally sat in until the last hand was played. I have never been what you could call a good poker player, but I tend to be lucky, which is even better. The old-timers in the outfit would lay in their beds and try to sleep while the rest of us played. That was no easy task; most of our games tended toward the raucous. Finally, some old puncher would lose his patience and threaten to go to shooting if some loud-mouth sons o' bitches didn't shut the hell up and blow out the lamp, and the game would end for the night.

Billy Christmas never took part in the card playing, but laid there in his soogans and thought his own thoughts until sleep overtook him. As it turned out, the boys who didn't play turned out to be the wise ones, but wisdom has little show when a feller's bent on having fun.

Doughbelly Pierce, the bean master I mentioned earlier, had the reputation of being cranky as a constipated bear, but he seemed to be in good humor that week. Every night, he brewed up a pot of strong black coffee for us poker players, and every night we drank the pot dry. I have to admit that after about the third day of trying to work those cowboy-broke horses on too little sleep I began to question Doughbelly's generosity some.

The coffee had another effect on some of us, especially me. It has been truly said that a man only *rents* coffee, and I was reminded of that truth one night about an hour after I'd fell asleep. At first I tried to keep snoozing and ignore my urgings, but they just came back stronger. Finally, I got up and stumbled out of the bunkhouse, hunting for relief.

There was a full moon that night, and a man could have read a book by its light. Moonlight flooded the land and dimmed the stars. Ranch buildings and corrals stood out clear as day, and I could even recognize some of the horses over in the catch pen beyond the barn. I was about to go back inside and take up sleeping again when a sudden movement caught my eye. Something had come gliding out of the trees up near the main house, a figure in white, running down the hill. *Julie!*

She had throwed on a coat, or maybe it was a shawl, over her nightgown, and she moved quickly, not looking back. Just as she reached the barn door a man stepped out to meet her, and I saw it was Billy Christmas. There could be no doubt. Billy took her in his arms, and I saw them kiss, then he turned and led her inside. All this happened in a flash. Had I been looking another way I'd have missed it altogether. I tried to tell myself I hadn't seen what I'd saw, that it was a trick of the moonlight and the shadows, but I knew the truth. I may not have been getting all the sleep I needed, but there was nothing wrong with my eyes. Back inside the bunkhouse, as I groped my way through the darkness I brushed my hand along Billy's bed. The canvas tarp was pulled up and smooth, but of course Billy was not there.

Back in my own bunk, I laid there and let my thoughts run. I can't say I was surprised by what I'd seen. The truth is, I'd have been surprised if Billy and Julie *hadn't* got together some time, some way. Whether it was love, lust, or locoweed that caused the pull between them I had no idea, but I knew it was Big Medicine, as the Indians say. Whatever it was, Billy and Julie seemed to be caught up in it like straws in a cyclone.

Sadness fell upon me like a cold, soggy blanket. Until that night I guess I had entertained some romantic hopes concerning Julie and myself. Now I have to admit that doing so required a fair amount of self deception, even for me. I had seen the way Julie looked at Billy, and there could be no doubt where her affections lay. Seeing them together by moonlight that evening laid the last of my fancies to rest.

I liked Billy and I more than liked Julie. I wished the best for them both, but I sure could see trouble ahead. I'm no fortune teller, but it didn't take a crystal ball to tell me Billy Christmas and Julie McAllister had got themselves rimrocked by their passion, with nowhere to go but over the edge and onto the boulders.

Sometimes, late at night, a man will let his dark thoughts stampede him, and he'll see things worse than they are. I tried to tell myself that was the case this time, but I knew better. All at once I went from feeling sorry for my friends to being downright hostile with them. How could they have done this to *me?* I hadn't asked to be put in a place of worry. I had no wish to see what I'd seen, know what I knew. And then the very foolishness of such thoughts made them collapse like a house of cards. Billy and Julie hadn't asked me to lose sleep over them. My state of mind was the last thing they were concerned about. I told myself to stop thinking about them and go to sleep, but I only thought about them even more. *Life isn't fair,* I thought. I remembered saying that once to a bartender over in Silver City. He'd looked wise as an owl and replied, *Nor will it ever be.* I hate it when bartenders are right.

In the week that followed, the rest of the roundup crew showed up. The nightly poker games continued as before, and the bunkhouse was filled with laughter, cuss words, and smoke. When the lamp finally went out and the boys were all bedded down, I'd lay there in my blankets and listen to the snoring and night sounds. I had cut back on my coffee drinking, but I still lay wakeful. This was not, as some might suppose, because I had a guilty conscience, but because my thoughts were of those who did, or leastways *should* have.

Three times that week I heard Billy get up and slip out into the darkness. I don't know how long he was away from the bunkhouse at those times; I drifted off to sleep before he came back. I was worried about my friends. It seemed to me they were riding a chancy trail with no way for the journey to end well, but I couldn't tell them that. If I had, they would likely have told me to mind my own business. And rightly so.

I took to helping Doughbelly put the final touches on his preparations. Together we mended harness, greased the hubs on the wagon wheels, and filled the chuck box with groceries and supplies. I put new shoes on the teams, fetched and carried, and generally tried to make myself useful. The M Cross wagon carried a two-day supply of water in a barrel attached to its side. Doughbelly asked me to fill the barrel with fresh water, and I said I would. I hitched the team to the wagon and drove it over to the good spring below the main house.

It was a pretty morning. A grove of aspens, their new leaves a-shimmer in the breeze, shaded the east side of the house. It was a warm day for May, and I noticed a couple of the windows facing the spring were open. From somewhere nearby I heard the call of a killdeer. Out on the flat a meadowlark sang. I bent to the spring and began to fill the keg. That's when I heard what I never meant to hear.

The sound of voices came from inside the house, one the deep, angry voice of Thane McAllister, the other, that of his daughter Julie. They were arguing, Thane laying down the law, and Julie defying him. At first I couldn't make out the words, only the anger and the bitterness. Then the words came, and before I could leave or declare my presence, I had heard too much. The day I had feared and expected had come.

"No, you will *not* marry that half-breed bronc stomper," Thane was saying, "not while *I* live! I have tolerated your wild misbehavior these past years, but I will *not* let you throw your life away!"

"I love him, daddy," Julie replied, "and nothing you say or do can change that! I'm going to marry Billy whether you approve or not!"

"Approve? How could I approve of my only daughter taking up with a cheap drifter like that, let alone talk of *marrying* him?"

"He's not a cheap drifter, daddy. He's a fine, decent man, and he loves me!"

"What he loves is your money—*my* money! By

god, I'm not turning the M Cross over to a gut-eatin' half breed!

"We don't want your money," Julie said. "You forget—I have money of my own—the twenty thousand mama left me."

"That trust fund is for your education, and for the time you marry a respectable man from a good family! You're a thoroughbred, and you weren't raised to run with the scrubs."

"We *are* scrubs, daddy!" Julie shouted. "You and mama started out poor and built what you have. Billy and I will do the same!"

"Your precious Billy will keep you barefoot and pregnant with little mixed-blood papooses while you cook for his drunken relatives! The answer is no, by god, and that's an end to it!"

I heard a door slam, the sound of a table or a chair falling somewhere inside, and then silence.

Everything happened fast after that. I drove the wagon back to where Doughbelly waited and went looking for Billy. I was on my way down to the corrals, where most of the other hands were, when Stub Peterson rode up and stopped me. Stub was wagon boss for the roundup that year, and he took his responsibility mighty serious. He looked puffed up and pompous as he pointed a stubby finger my way. "The outfit's leavin', Fanshaw," he said. "Roll your bed, get mounted, and jingle them saddlehorses out on the trail. We'll camp at Coyote Flats this evenin'."

My nod told him I would. "By the bye, Stub," I said, "you don't know where I can find Billy Christmas, do you?"

Stub scratched his belly and spat. "Billy's gone," he said. "Rode out early this mornin' with Waco Calhoun and Red Murphy. Billy was ridin' that gray of his and leadin' his packhorse. I don't expect he'll be comin' back."

I felt like I'd swallowed a cold rock. "No," I said, "I don't expect he will."

three

The roundup went off slicker than calf slobbers. By day I herded the remuda and did what I could to give Doughbelly a hand. I helped hitch and load the wagons, helped set up and take down the camp, and rustled wood and water. When there was no wood I gathered dry cow chips in a gunny sack and fetched them back to the wagon. Doughbelly teased me some about that last duty—called it "picking flowers"—but he was mighty glad to have the fuel. Once or twice, when he had his hands full, I wound up peeling spuds and making coffee.

Helping the cook was part of the job, but my main duty was herding the horses. I kept them on good grass, saw they were well-watered and waiting when the boys were ready to change mounts. The nighthawk was an old-timer I'd knowed since I was just a button, and I turned the ponies over to him at sundown. Then I et supper with the punchers and bedded down until first light, when the whole process began again.

Sometimes I'd pass the time of day with one or another of the boys, and I'd ask about Billy Christmas. Nobody had seen him since the day he rode out with Waco and Red, or had any idea as to his whereabouts. I stayed curious, but uninformed.

The rains came late that spring, starting about mid-June and soaking the range and all that was on it, including us cowpunchers. Most of us had some kind of saddle slicker, but those oilskins never really kept us dry. Our bedrolls stayed damp, as well, which made for some miserable nights. I almost came to believe being cold and wet was a permanent condition. When pulling my boots on I even checked to make sure I hadn't growed webbed feet.

It was still raining when Stub Peterson pulled the wagons back to the home ranch the last week of June. Waco Calhoun paid us off, and we all rode away to our different destinations. As for me, I lit out for Dry Creek with the intention of sleeping until my next birthday. Because I had worked off and on at the Dry Creek livery, I paid a call on the widow Blair, who owned the place. She allowed that if I'd pitch in and help out part-time, I could board my horses there and sleep in the loft. I told her that suited me right down to the ground.

The rain continued to fall, as though someone up yonder had forgot to turn off the spigot. I remember hoping the Almighty hadn't turned absent-minded, although if he had it would have explained some of the prayers I'd not had an answer to. I took my bedroll apart in the stable's office, shook out the sagebrush, twigs, and spiders, and dried my blankets in front of the stove. Then I lugged everything up to the loft, built myself a nest in the driest corner I could find, and slept for sixteen hours straight.

Once I'd caught up on my rest some, I sauntered into Ignacio's Cafe and ordered most of what was written in the bill of fare. Owing to the lateness of the hour, the place was nearly empty. Ignacio was glad to see me.

"Hola, amigo," he said. "I heard you was back. You came to town for a decent meal, no?"

I grinned at him. "No," I said, "I came to find out if your cooking has improved any. I keep hoping."

Ignacio shrugged. "I make a living," he said, "and I don' have to chase no dam' cows in the rain, neither."

By the time I'd worked my way through a T-bone steak, fried taters and gravy, corn with chiles, three or four biscuits, and a slab of peach pie I found I had pretty well ruined my appetite. Full as a tick, I slumped back in my chair and watched Ignacio refill my coffee cup. He drawed out the chair across from me and sat down.

"What's new in town?" I asked him. "I feel like I've been gone for a year."

Ignacio rolled a corn-shuck cigarita and set fire to it. He shrugged again. "*Nada*," he said. "Nothing changes in Dry Creek."

Ignacio looked thoughtful. For a time he smoked in silence, blue smoke writhing up toward the low ceiling. Then he said, "Homer Hess got drunk and beat up his missus again. She got even, though. Broke his leg with a sledge hammer while he was passed out."

Ignacio laughed. "Sheepherder took his dog with him into Jackrabbit Annie's whorehouse last week. Dog bit one of the customers. Customer was the circuit judge. Now the sheepherder's doin' thirty days in the *calabozo*."

I laughed, too. "You're right," I said. "Nothing changes in Dry Creek."

Ignacio stood, walked to the door, and flipped the cigarita out into the muddy street. When he came back, he said, "One strange thing, amigo. Two weeks ago, just before the rain, some boys found an hombre—a stranger— outside of town. Someone had beat him nearly to death and left him tied to a tree. It was *muy malo*—very bad."

"Robbery?"

"No. His saddlehorse and packhorse were tied nearby. And he had *mucho dinero*—five hundred dollars in a money belt. Glenn Murdoch took him to Doc Taggart's office. Afterward, this hombre paid Doc and rode south, out of town."

43

"Did he say who beat him?"

"No. He tol' Glenn it was *nada*. A fight among friends."

"Well, who was he? Didn't anybody ask his name?"

"*Por supuesto*. Of course. A funny name, he had. He said his name is Billy Christmas."

I've already told you about Glenn Murdoch, the undersheriff. I went directly from Ignacio's to Glenn's office to pay my respects and to ask a few questions. Glenn was glad to see me. For one thing, he liked playing cards to pass the time, and he liked playing with me especially because I mostly lost.

You recall when I said I'm not a good poker player but that I tend to be lucky? Well, for some reason that don't seem to apply much to cribbage, a game at which I'm neither skilled *nor* lucky.

Anyway, as soon as he saw me Glenn told me to take my boots off outside so as not to track up his floor. Then he reached into his desk for the crib board and the cards.

"Cut them pasteboards," he said. "In case you've forgotten, low card deals. Let's see if your game has improved any since last time."

It hadn't. I lost two straight games and was riding drag in the third when I brought up the question of Billy Christmas.

"Ignacio told me about the feller the boys found whipped and tied to a tree," I said. "I understand he gave his name as Billy Christmas."

Glenn was all lawman, from his belt buckle both ways. He fixed me with a cool, official stare that asked why I'd raised the subject. "Yes," he said. "He told me he'd been riding the rough string out at the M Cross. I expect you knew him there."

"Knew him and liked him. I was wondering if you had any idea who worked him over and why."

Glenn studied me for a moment across the cards he held and said, "He told me it was nothing, just a fight with some friends. He wouldn't give me their names so I took a ride out to the M Cross. Thane McAllister told me he'd paid Billy off and set him on the road to Dry Creek in the company of Waco Calhoun and Red Murphy. McAllister didn't say why."

I picked up my cards and played an eight. "Could be it had something to do with Thane's daughter Julie," I said. "She had eyes for Billy, and the feeling was mutual. I figure Thane wanted Billy off the ranch."

Glenn played a seven on my eight and pegged two points. I could feel his eyes on me like sunbeams through a magnifying glass. "Say more," he said.

"I also figure Thane wanted Billy to be plum' certain he wasn't welcome at the M Cross, so he had Waco and Red make the message crystal clear." I paired Glenn's seven and scored two points myself.

"That's what I figured, too," Glenn said. "Waco and Red admitted they'd rode with him to Dry Creek, but that was all. I couldn't prove they'd worked him over, and Billy just kept saying he'd been in a fight with friends.

"Strange kind of fight, though. When I took Billy down to Doc Taggart's that day he had cuts and bruises from one end to the other. Even had a broken nose. You want to know the one part of him that *wasn't* beat up? His *knuckles,* Merlin. Waco and Red beat hell out of that boy, but he didn't fight back. I figure they didn't give him the chance."

"But if you know—"

"Law don't care what I know. Law cares what I can prove. But I'm a patient man. Some day, some time, Thane McAllister will have to account for that beating."

Glenn played a third seven and pegged six points. "Go," I told him, and derned if he didn't play the case seven for twelve points and another one for go. Cribbage just isn't my game.

The following day I was back playing cards with Glenn again. That's the day I told you about when Delbert Snodgrass rode off into the gumbo and Glenn volunteered me to fetch him back. As you may recall, Delbert mentioned Billy Christmas at that time and asked if I'd met him. That's when I wandered off the main trail, made a short story long, and told you pretty much all I knowed about Billy, Thane McAllister, and Julie.

The rain eased off to a drizzle and finally quit. The sun came out and dried up the countryside. The prairie turned green as ever it gets, wildflowers bloomed, and the cry of the curlew was heard in the land. Glenn turned Delbert loose, and the hard-luck desperado saddled his glass-eyed pony and loped off to a better life, or anyway I hoped he did.

I cleaned stalls at the livery stable and helped Bummer, the night man, patch holes in the roof. The widow Blair bought a ton of first cutting hay from a homesteader east of town, and Bummer and me put it up in the barn loft for her. The widow baked me a pie—rhubarb, it was—and I et everything but the pie tin it came in. Whiskey and women were never my weaknesses—well, at least *whiskey* wasn't—but I believe under the right circumstances I might have committed treason for a fresh-baked rhubarb pie.

The weather turned hot, and I took to stopping at the Oasis Saloon for a beer along about mid-afternoon. Boogles, the owner, was a disagreeable old skinflint, but he cut ice every winter from a nearby slough and kept it packed in sawdust for the summer trade, so the beer was always cold.

I was standing at the long bar one day, nursing my brew and trying to get a rise out of Boogles, when Stub Peterson, wagon boss for the M Cross, ambled in and set his elbows on the hardwood. "Gimme a beer," he told Boogles, "and bring Merlin here another one."

"Much obliged, Stub," I said, "How've you been?"

"Too damn hot. Other'n that, I can't complain."

Boogles drawed a pair of cold ones and set them before us. Stub drank half of his and licked the foam off his moustache. "Thane took the notion to put up hay this summer out to the ranch," he said, "Hayin' is thirsty work."

I nodded. "How is Thane?" I asked, "and Julie?"

"Thane? Same as ever, I guess. Julie, too, far as I know."

"She still at the ranch then?"

"Hell yes, she's still at the ranch. Where else would she be?"

I took a sip of my beer and tried to look casual. "Nowheres, I guess. I just thought maybe she'd gone back to school or something."

"Let me give you a little free advice, Merlin. Try not to think about Julie so much. Young bucks thinkin' about Julie tend to make Thane nervous."

I finished my beer and set the stein back on the bar. "I figure free advice is just about worth the price," I told him. I bought him a beer, we talked cattle prices and the weather for awhile, and I headed on back to the livery barn. Thinking about Julie tended to make *me* nervous, too, in a pleasant kind of way.

I continued to see Glenn a couple of times a week, but he never mentioned Billy Christmas again, and I didn't bring the subject up either. I guess we both figured there was nothing more to say, and we had the good sense not to keep a-saying it.

Glenn had a new problem on his mind, anyway. "The Coldwater gang is operating in our area again," he said, "They robbed the Merchant's Bank in Silver City last week. Shot the teller."

"The Coldwater gang!" says I. "I thought they'd left this country—I heard they'd gone down to Oklahoma or somewheres."

"I heard that, too," said Glenn. "Wherever they went, they're back now. Witnesses at Silver City saw Vince and Cletus Coldwater plain as day. Vince's common-law wife Ramona was with them, too."

"That is bad news," I said, "but Silver City is twenty miles away, and in another county. There's no call for you to be concerned just yet."

Glenn fixed me with a cold stare and raised one eyebrow higher than the other. "The Coldwater gang is cause for concern wherever it is," he said.

Over the next few weeks I commenced to grow restive. I worked my horses some. I read my favorite books over again and borrowed others from people I knowed around town. I even read some of Glenn's law books. My sometime lady friend Pandora Pretty Hawk was away, visiting her people on the reservation, and I missed her. I wrote her three letters. I even mailed one of them.

When I'd talked with Stub Peterson that day at the Oasis, he had offered me a riding job with the M Cross, but not until fall. The widow Blair allowed me to board my horses and sleep at the livery in exchange for part-time work, but there were no wages involved. And anyway, it don't take long for harness mending, rat killing, and shoveling horse poop to lose their appeal. The widow did pay me two dollars to whitewash her picket fence, and I did that. I spent one dollar on beer, and squandered the rest on food.

It wasn't only that my ready cash was running out. I found myself wearied by the sameness of Dry Creek and its doings. I longed to meet new people and see new places. I hankered for excitement and adventure—anything to break the monotony.

A man really should be careful what he hankers for.

I have always been partial to buckskin horses. Now I know what you're going to say. You're going to tell me that what color a horse is has nothing to do with how good it is, and I allow you have a point. But a man's ideas and notions are based on his experience, and the best horse I ever owned was a buckskin. I called him Little Buck, and he was tough, willing, and smart. He had what the old-timers call bottom, which means he would never shirk, even when the going was at its toughest, and that there was no quit to him at all.

Anyway, along about the end of March I picked up this three-year-old buckskin gelding in a horse trade, and the animal confirmed my good opinion of the color and reinforced my prejudices. I named him Rutherford, after Rutherford B. Hayes, who was a better president than folks give him credit for, even if he *did* steal the election back in '76.

I had been working with Rutherford out on the big sagebrush flat west of town, roping off him and training him to stand steady no matter what I dabbed my rope on. I would drop a noose on one of those big old sagebrushes, take my dallies, and pop the bush out of the ground like pulling a tooth. The first few times I tried that made Rutherford nervous, and one day he even fell to bucking with me. But he soon growed accustomed to the rope and took the whole process in his stride. I believe I could have roped a grizzly bear off him without too much trouble, at least until after I'd made the catch.

I was riding Rutherford back into town one morning after our roping practice and had occasion to pass Glenn's office as I did so. It was then I noticed the leggy black Morgan tied to the hitchrack out front. I would have knowed that horse out of a thousand, and seeing him brought back memories of the times I'd seen him before and the man who rode him: U.S. Marshal Chance Ridgeway.

I have to admit I was curious. I wasn't but eighteen when I first met the old lawman, but we'd shared some times that year that were anything but dull. I figured he was in town to discuss legal business with Glenn. I knowed I had no call to butt in, but the marshal was an old acquaintance. Maybe, I told myself, he'd even be glad to see me. Anyway, I figured talking with him again might at least relieve the boredom for awhile. I stepped down off Rutherford, tied him alongside the Morgan, and went inside.

The marshal was seated across the desk from Glenn. They both looked up, surprised like, when I came in. I figured I had broke in on some serious talk between them, so I got started on my apology right away. "Howdy, Glenn," I said. "Good morning, Marshal. Sorry to interrupt you gents, but I saw your horse out yonder and thought I'd pay my respects."

Ridgeway hadn't changed much. He was lean and gangly as a sandhill crane, and his faded blue eyes were lively and knowing. Beneath the snowy white of his handlebar moustache, a grin was forming. "Merlin Fanshaw," he drawled. "Well, I declare. Where have you been a-keepin' yourself, son?"

"Around Dry Creek here, mostly," I told him. "I wrangled horses for the M Cross during spring roundup. You're lookin' good, marshal."

The blue eyes twinkled. "You mean I'm lookin' good for an old man pushin' sixty," he said.

"No such a thing," I said. "Besides, sixty ain't old."

"It ain't old, for a *tree*. Pull up a chair and join us, young Merlin. It may surprise you some, but one reason I'm here in Dry Creek is to see you."

It did surprise me. I glanced at Glenn, who nodded, then looked down at his hands. I drug a chair over and straddled it. I searched my recent past for some wrong-doing worthy of a U.S. Marshal's attention, but could think of none.

"You may recall that I once offered you a deputy's badge," Ridgeway said. "I'm here to make that offer again."

"I don't hardly know what to say, marshal. It ain't that I don't appreciate the offer," I said, "but I'm no lawman. Ask Glenn."

"Already have. He figures you can fill the bill."

I recalled my recent longings for action and adventure. I stuck my hand in my pants pocket and found mostly lint. I surely could use a job, and no mistake. But as a deputy U.S. Marshal?

"I don't have no idea what the job requires," I said. "What would I need to do?"

"Pretty much whatever I tell you to," Ridgeway said. "Most deputies work on a fee basis, but Uncle Sam tends to be a mite slow to settle his accounts. I pay my deputies a straight salary against fees while they're waitin', plus expenses. I'll start you at two dollars a day."

Ridgeway stood up from his chair, unfolding his lanky frame like a carpenter's rule. His spurs chimed softly as he walked to the window and looked out. "As it happens, I already have an assignment for you," he said. "I'd need you to start right away." For a long moment the old lawman was silent, his back to Glenn and me. Then he turned and met my gaze. "It appears," he said, "that the Coldwater gang has kidnapped Julie McAllister."

four

Silence fell upon the room like a fist. I had heard Ridgeway's words, but I could not get my mind around them. I stared at the old marshal's face, then shifted my glance to Glenn. *Julie kid-*

53

napped! Maybe, I thought, this was some kind of foolery on Ridgeway's part, a joke shared by him and Glenn that had somehow went over my head. But the faces that met my gaze were serious as a banker's funeral. Ridgeway had meant exactly what he'd said.

From the inside pocket of his coat he produced a folded paper and carefully opened it. "This telegram came to my office in Silver City yesterday," he said. He cleared his throat, held the paper out at arm's length, and read:

NEED YOUR HELP.
MY DAUGHTER JULIE KIDNAPPED.
PLEASE COME MY RANCH SOONEST.
THANE.

Glenn nodded. "I saw Thane coming out of the telegraph office here yesterday," he said. "He looked like a man with a troubled mind. But he didn't say a word about any of this to me."

Ridgeway carefully folded the paper again and put it away, inside his coat. "That surprise you, does it? Next to the word 'proud' in the dictionary is a picture of Thane McAllister."

Glenn nodded. "And another picture of him next to the word 'stubborn'," he said, "but he might have mentioned his problem. I do keep the law hereabouts."

"And you do a fine job," Ridgeway said, "but Thane and me have known each other for twenty years or more. I stood up with him when he married Lucinda, and I'm Julie's godfather. It's only natural he'd come to me first."

"Hell, Chance, I know that. Besides which, you're federal law while I'm local. All men may be created equal, like they say, but Thane McAllister figures he's just a little *more* equal than everybody else. He just naturally believes he's entitled to the best."

"If you know that about Thane, you know how hard it was for him to ask anyone for help. He likes to handle things himself."

Glenn looked like he had plenty more to say on the subject, but he held his tongue. All he said was, "Yes. He sure as hell does."

"In any case," Ridgeway said, "I wanted you to know. I'll be going out to the M Cross from here. You're more than welcome to ride along."

Glenn shook his head. "I appreciate the offer, but no. It's you he asked for. Let me know if there's anything I can do."

"I will keep you informed," Ridgeway said.

Marshal Ridgeway turned his attentions back to me. "Well, Merlin?" he said. "I seem to recall making you an offer."

The marshal stood with his back to the window, his face deep-shadowed against the brightness. I met his gaze. "All right," I told him. "You've hired yourself a deputy. But any time you figure I ain't making a hand, just let me know. I'll roll my bed and draw my time."

Ridgeway's smile was warm as summer. "I expect you'll do just fine," he said.

Out on the street I kept glancing down at the badge Ridgeway had pinned to my vest. Sunlight kept a-winking off its nickel-plated surface, and I got so busy trying to see myself reflected in the window glass that I stumbled off the boardwalk and nearly fell. I looked at Ridgeway out of the corner of my eye, but he didn't appear to have noticed.

It seems like every cow outfit has one puncher who spends most of his pay to deck himself out in the fanciest duds money can buy. Cowpunchers are proud of their trade, and some of them like to show off that pride in their rigging. Because they don't spend much time around mirrors, these Fancy Dans get in the habit of watching their shadows as they ride along. A man will set tall in the saddle with his shoulders throwed back, admiring his silhouette as it slides over the grass. Most of the time there ain't any harm in the practice, but every now and then one of them shadow riders will miss seeing a stray steer or a badger hole and get himself into a jackpot. That's sort of the way I felt about me and my new badge, and I was thankful my foolishness had gone unobserved. At least I hoped it had.

Ridgeway backed his long-legged Morgan away from the hitchrack and stepped into the saddle. I swung up on Rutherford, and the marshal and me set out on the road to the M Cross.

The news of Julie's kidnapping had hit me like a bucket of ice water. I had a hundred questions, but Ridgeway was short on answers. "All I know is what Thane wrote in his telegram," he said. "I expect we'll learn more when we talk to him."

We rode north out of Dry Creek, following the wagon road that cut through the long sagebrush flats. By noon we had crossed the west fork of Brimstone Creek and turned up into the stands of aspen that led to the ranch. A rising breeze set the leaves to pattering and sighed through the tops of the dog-hair pines beyond. Ridgeway and me rode in silence, each alone with our thoughts. The marshal had made it clear he wasn't interested in answering my questions right then so I didn't ask any, but I sure did have a few.

I thought about Julie and wondered where she was right then. In my mind's eye she was dressed the way I remembered her, sleek black hair cascading down below the brim of her pearl gray Stetson, white shirt beneath her black wool vest, red silk scarf loose-knotted about her slender neck. I recalled the way the hem of her riding skirt fell just below her calves, and how her hand-made boots showed off her tiny feet. Mostly, I remembered her dark eyes and the sadness I'd seen there, a lonesome sorrow that made a man hurt just to see it. Was she frightened now? Had her kidnappers treated her decently or had they abused her?

Back at Dry Creek Ridgeway had said he had a job

for me, that he needed me right away. He had sworn me in as a deputy U.S. Marshal, he had bade me ride with him to the M Cross and a meeting with Thane McAllister, but he'd said nothing more. What did he have in mind? Was I to be part of some plan to rescue Julie? I had questions aplenty, but answers seemed scarce as fur on a hog.

It was late afternoon when we broke out of the trees and turned our horses through the ranch gate. Ahead lay the familiar buildings: the big house up the hill, the bunkhouse, blacksmith shop, horse barn, and corrals below. The rumble of our horses' hooves rang hollow on the bridge planks over Little Otter Creek, and then Ridgeway and me turned up toward the house.

As we approached, Thane McAllister stepped out onto the veranda. He was the same as I remembered him, yet not the same. He was still bigger than life, but he no longer carried himself as if he held title deed to the world. He wore a three-day beard, and his clothes had a rumpled, slept-in look. He gave Ridgeway a rueful smile as the marshal drew rein, but I don't believe he saw me at all.

Waco Calhoun did, though. The M Cross foreman stood in the doorway behind Thane, thumbs hooked in his gun belt, watching me. His face showed only cool speculation, but I knew he'd seen my deputy's badge and was wondering how the outfit's horse wrangler had suddenly turned lawman.

Thane met Marshal Ridgeway at the front steps.

The two men shook hands, gratitude plain on the cattleman's face. "Much obliged for coming, Chance," McAllister said. "I knew you would."

"Yes," said Ridgeway, "I'm sorry for your trouble, Thane."

Ridgeway turned to me. "I guess you know my deputy," he said. "Merlin just signed on to help me keep the law."

McAllister looked confused. He looked at the badge, then at me, trying to place me. I helped him out. "Merlin Fanshaw, Mr. McAllister," I said. "I wrangled horses for you on the roundup this spring."

Recognition came suddenly. "I remember you," he said. "You did a good job." He took Ridgeway's arm and led him toward the entryway. "Come on inside," he said.

Waco stepped away from the door, his eyes still on me. "So you're working for the law now," he said. I was thinking about Billy Christmas, tied to a tree and beaten half to death, when I answered him. "Yes. I figure this country *needs* more law—you know, to protect *travelers* and such."

Inside the ranch house, Thane led us to a cluster of chairs in front of a big, stone fireplace. Beyond the hearth, flames flickered and snapped, casting shadows across the room. Thane waited until the marshal and me sat down, then eased his bulk into an oversized wing chair. He sat there for a moment, drumming his fingers on the arm of the chair as he looked me over. Then he turned to Ridgeway.

"Meanin' no offense, Chance," he said, "but does Fanshaw need to be here? I thought it would be just you and me."

I started to get up and leave the room, but Ridgeway put his hand out and stopped me. "No offense taken," he drawled, "but we're on official business, here to talk about a serious crime. My deputy stays."

Thane nodded, looking at the floor. "All right," he said.

He raised his head, looking at nothing, remembering. Then, with a long sigh, he began. "Day before yesterday Julie took her mare out to ride the meadows above the ranch. When she didn't come back at noon I figured she'd taken a lunch and planned to spend her day up in the hills. She did that sometimes. Liked to be by herself. Now and again she'd take a book with her. She would set under a tree and read some. Other times she'd just ride the country up there.

"When she wasn't back at sundown I rode out to look for her." Thane closed his eyes and fell silent for a time. Then he cleared his throat and said, "I found no trace of her, or her horse. I did find her neck scarf, though. It was tied like a flag to the low branch of a blue spruce."

Thane picked up a folded paper from the table beside his chair. His face showed no expression at all, but I noticed his hand trembled as he handed the paper to Ridgeway. "This note was with it," he said.

Marshal Ridgeway opened the paper, looked at it,

and handed it to me. The words had been printed in pencil in big, block letters:

TO THANE MCALLISTER

WEV GOT YUR DAUTER. IF YOU WANT HER BACK ALIVE BRING $10,000 TO POINT OF ROCKS 8 OCLOCK FRIDY NIGHT.

LEAVE MONEY IN FORKS OF DEAD TREE.

CUM ALONE. NO TRICKS. WE MEAN BISNESS!

VINCE & CLETUS COLDWATER

Ridgeway sat straight-backed in his chair, his hands on his knees. For a time, the only sound was the ticking of the Regulator clock on the wall beside the fireplace. Then Ridgeway said, "Them damn Coldwaters are a bunion on the big toe of decency. Did you do what they asked?"

A shadow seemed to pass over Thane's face. He shrugged and lowered his eyes. "Point of Rocks is maybe five miles from here, where Brimstone Creek flows into the Little Porcupine. There's a limestone outcropping there where the river bends and a standing dead cottonwood on the bank."

Thane's voice took on a hard edge. There was anger in his tone, but pain as well. "I took the money from my safe—ten thousand dollars in greenbacks—but I wasn't about to let them damned kidnappers call the turn. I told Stub Peterson and Red Murphy to get their guns and come with me.

"Told 'em to keep back out of sight while I put the

61

money in the tree, but to come a-runnin' when I called.

"When I got to Point of Rocks I didn't see anyone. It was a dark night, overcast, and the shadows were black there beside the river. I waited maybe five minutes, then I did what the note said—hung the money in the forks of that old cottonwood. I waited maybe an hour longer, but saw nobody. No Coldwaters. No Julie."

"What about Stub and Red?" I asked.

Thane looked subdued. He lowered his eyes and stared at the floor. His voice was a hoarse growl when he answered. "They didn't see a thing. After awhile, they came down to find me, but it was too late. Somehow, the Coldwaters had slipped up in the dark and had made off with the money. They didn't give Julie back, of course."

The big cattleman leaned forward in his chair, his eyes on Ridgeway. "I made a botch of it, Chance," he said. "I kept thinking about those damn outlaws putting their hands on my girl, taking her prisoner and all, and I just got mad!" He was silent for a moment. His voice was low and full of regret as he said, "I shouldn't have took the boys with me."

"Spilled milk," Ridgeway said. "You saw nobody?"

Thane shook his head. "No," he said, "but when daylight came we found their tracks. There were three of 'em. Two men and a boy, by their bootprints. They crossed the Little Porcupine and headed east."

Thane's face was open as a child's. "You don't

reckon they'll do her hurt because I didn't follow their orders, do you?"

"No," Ridgeway said. "Them boys are playing a high-stakes game, and Julie is their trade goods. You'll be hearing from them again."

Ridgeway stood up, and I followed suit. So did Thane McAllister. "We'd like to look around some," Ridgeway said, "if that'd be all right. Maybe look at Julie's room, talk to Red and Stub. We could use a picture of Julie, if you have one."

Thane nodded. "Whatever you need. She had her photograph made while she was back east. I'll get it for you."

When Thane left the room to get the photograph, Ridgeway turned his attention to me. "Well, deputy?" he asked, "What do you think?"

"Like you said. The kidnappers will come at Thane again, and soon."

"Yes," Ridgeway said, "I believe they will."

I had learned during the roundup that Doughbelly Pierce was a fine cook, but he outdid himself that evening. He served up a spread of liver and onions with peas and new potatoes in pan gravy that would have made my friend Ignacio jealous. Fact is, I had to go back for seconds twice just to be sure the grub was really as good as it seemed. After supper, Ridgeway and me talked awhile with Stub Peterson and Red Murphy, but they added nothing to Thane's story.

63

Back at the main house, Thane broke out the good bourbon and poured the marshal and me three fingers of whiskey each. I seldom drink hard liquor, but I figured that under the circumstances it wouldn't be polite to say no. For a time, we just sat there and watched the fire. Nobody spoke. Then Thane turned to face Ridgeway. "Well, Chance?" he said. "What do you think I ought to do?"

There was sympathy in Ridgeway's voice when he replied. "The hardest thing there is to do," he said. "Wait."

Thane scowled. "Taking orders from those damned Coldwaters don't set well with me," he said. "I ain't much in a mood for waiting."

His jaw took on a stubborn set. "I could put twenty armed men on their trail in an hour," he said, "men that would track those bastards down if it took a year."

"I expect you could," said Ridgeway, "if you were willing to take the risk. But it's a rare posse that will stick with a trail for long. They get to thinking about soft beds, saloons, and womenfolk, start arguing among themselves."

Doubt flickered across Thane's face with the firelight. He brought his fist down hard on the arm of his chair. "Damn it!" he said. "A man has to do something!"

"Yes," Ridgeway agreed. "Right now a man has to wait."

64

Marshal Ridgeway and me stayed the night in a guest room at the main house instead of the bunkhouse where I was accustomed to spreading my blankets. I laid awake and thought about Julie some, wondering where she might be and hoping she was all right. I even tried praying, but I couldn't recall the store-bought prayers I'd learned at Sunday school, and the one my mother had taught me about "Now I Lay Me Down to Sleep" didn't seem to fit the occasion. Finally, I just asked the Almighty to watch over Julie and keep her safe, and I fell asleep hoping He would.

Come morning, I saddled Ridgeway's Morgan and my horse Rutherford, and we made ready for the ride back to Dry Creek. I couldn't get over the way losing Julie had broke Thane McAllister down. Thane was a proud man, and he had walked the earth with his head high. Now his shoulders slumped and his eyes were red-rimmed as a hound's, watery and lifeless. I never thought I'd feel sorry for the richest man in Progress County, but I found to my surprise that I did. Thane had been the great he-bull of the territory, but now he looked lost and lonesome as a dogie calf with the scours.

Down at the barn Ridgeway took Thane aside. I don't know if I was supposed to, but I overheard their conversation. "I'm taking Merlin down south of Dry Creek to pick up a tracker and a pack outfit," the marshal said. "Can you put the boys up when they get back?"

"Of course," Thane said. He looked intently at Ridgeway, questions in his eyes. "You said a tracker. Anyone I know?"

"I expect you've heard of him. Hoodoo Hawks. Indian scout, prospector, range detective, and the best trailsman I know. The man can track bees through a blizzard."

"When he's sober, maybe," Thane said. "From what I hear, that's a rare condition for him these days. But all right, if you say so. Then what?"

"Then you wait for word from the kidnappers. When you hear from them, do what they tell you, pay what they ask, and keep your head. Once you get Julie back, my deputy and Hawks will take the trail and track the scoundrels down."

We left the ranch in the cool of the morning, pausing a mile below the ranch to water our horses. Ridgeway's Morgan stretched his neck out over Little Otter Creek and drank like a gentleman, sucking deep drafts of water in through nearly closed lips. My horse was nowhere near so refined. Rutherford stumbled off the rocky bank, splashing out upstream of the Morgan and muddying the creek as he slurped up water with many a noisy gulp and swaller. If Ridgeway noticed Rutherford's rudeness he made no mention of it.

"I found your plans for my future mighty interesting," I told Ridgeway, "especially since I only just learned about them when you told Thane."

"I'm sorry if your feelings are hurt," the marshal

said, "but if you recall, I told you the job of deputy was pretty much whatever I said it was. Do you have a problem with that?"

"I reckon not. But I am curious. Who is this Hoodoo Hawks you've paired me with?"

"Like I told Thane—he's a former Indian scout, prospector, and range detective—and the best tracker in the territory. Lives in the badlands south of Dry Creek."

"If he's so all-fired famous, how come I never heard of him?"

"I can't say. Maybe you've neglected your education."

"Yeah. Well, I ain't real sure I want to pardner with some burned out boozer from the olden times."

Ridgeway gave me a tolerant grin. " 'Want to' don't enter into it, son," he said. "Either you will, or you can go back to shoveling horseshit at the livery barn. As for Hoodoo, I don't expect *he'll* be all that anxious to team up with *you*."

I turned Rutherford away from the creek and set him on the road to Dry Creek. "Well, I'm sure you'll talk him into it," I huffed. "You do have persuadin' ways."

five

West of Dry Creek the land rolls away toward the mountains in one long stretch of weathered coulees and sun-scorched draws. Bunch grass clings to the bottoms and waits for rains that seldom come. Greasewood and sagebrush, twisted by the wind, offer scant shade for lizard and snake, and bare patches of red dirt shimmer in the heat waves. We followed no trail I could make out, yet Ridgeway rode out across the badlands like a sea captain sure of his course.

Growing up around Dry Creek, I had come to know the area somewhat, although not nearly so well as I pretended. I had been in that region now and again, searching for missing horses or hunting deer, but the range was poor and waterless. I figured there was little reason for a man or his critters to go there.

So it was that a mile later, when Ridgeway turned his Morgan down a steep game trail and into a timbered hollow, I expected nothing in particular. I have to admit I was some surprised when we broke out of a cedar patch and came suddenly upon a cabin at the foot of a green and grassy defile. The cabin was sod-roofed and low to the ground, set back near a spring among the cedars. At a pole corral a hundred yards beyond, two horses—a sorrel and a paint—watched our approach. The sorrel whinnied a shrill greeting, and my horse Rutherford whinnied back as if he thought we had appointed him our spokesman. From behind the cabin a lanky, blue-haired hound trotted stiffly toward us, barking his challenge and causing Rutherford to go into a nervous quickstep. Ever the gentleman, Ridgeway's Morgan ignored the dog, moved on up to the cabin, and stopped, facing the door.

"Hello the house!" Ridgeway called. "It's me, Chance Ridgeway! Call off your pot-hound."

The cabin door opened a crack, then wider. Out into the sunlight stepped a man of about fifty, a Winchester rifle held at the ready. "Dog," he said quietly, and the hound turned from tormenting my horse and trotted, tail wagging, back to the cabin.

The man I took to be Hoodoo Hawks was small in stature, lean and leathery. Shoulder length gray hair hung lank from beneath a battered hat, and his face was dark from sun and wind. At some time in the past his nose had been broken, more than once from the look of it. It had a reddish cast, and there was high color in his cheeks as well. The man carried himself with the stiff concentration of a drinker well into his cups, and a vagrant breeze brought the smell of whiskey all the way from where he stood.

I noticed that he carried his left arm in a makeshift sling. He wore a buckskin coat, with breed leggings and mocassins, and he carried a Bowie knife and a six-gun on a belt about his waist. He took a careful step toward Ridgeway, head thrust forward, eyes squinting, as if to be certain the marshal really was who he said he was. Satisfied, he greeted the lawman with a reluctant nod. "Marshal," he said.

For a long moment Hawks studied Ridgeway. Then he turned away, his eyes on me. He was talking to Ridgeway but looking at me when he said, "You're runnin' with a younger crowd these days, Marshal. Who's the pup?"

"The 'pup' can talk," I told him. "I'm Merlin Fanshaw, from Dry Creek, and I'm the marshal's new deputy. Who the hell are you?"

Hawks ignored me. "First baby lawman I ever seen," he told Ridgeway. "Have you boys et?"

"We have not," said Ridgeway. "You asking us to supper?"

"I expect. Get down and come inside."

Ridgeway stepped down stiffly from the Morgan. He loosened the saddle cinch, slipped off the bridle, and turned his horse loose. I hobbled Rutherford and did likewise, and the ponies took to grazing on the tall grass behind the cabin.

By the time I ducked under the doorway and stepped inside, Ridgeway had already taken the only chair. Hawks pulled the cork on a whiskey jug and offered it to the marshal. Ridgeway took a long swig, handed it back, and smoothed his moustache. His expression gave no clue as to the whiskey's quality, but he seemed to have trouble catching his breath and his right eye had begun to twitch. I halfway expected him to commence vibrating and explode.

70

Hawks then handed the jug to me. As I've said, I never was much of a drinking man. I expect I'd seen too much of my pa's struggle with whiskey for it to have much appeal for me. Besides, I always figured life is hard enough to deal with when a man's in his *right* mind. Still, the conventions of the time required a man to take a drink when offered one, so I took a pull on the jug and handed it back. Hawks nodded, took a long drink himself, and the ceremonials were completed. Sort of like smoking a peace pipe with an Indian chief. Hawks turned his back on me and went to building up the fire in his cookstove.

Now I have to admit I was feeling a mite ringy right then. I had been called a "pup" and a "baby lawman" and I was half past surly and a quarter to mad as hell. Worst of all, I felt that Hawks was looking down his busted red nose at me, as if I was too piddling to take notice of. I was about to call him on his rude attitude when Ridgeway took up the subject. "I don't hardly feel you and my deputy have been properly intro-duced," he told Hawks. "One reason we've come here is so you boys can get acquainted."

Hawks greased a skillet with a piece of bacon rind and laid in three thick steaks. He did not look my way. "I guess I've seen what I need to," he said.

His back was turned to me, so that's what I spoke to. "I hope your eyesight is better than your man-ners," I told him. "You ain't really looked at me yet."

The steaks sizzled on the stove. Hawks still didn't

turn around, but tended to his cooking. "A man don't *need* to do much lookin' once he's learned how to *see*," he said. "You're twenty, maybe twenty-one years old, you weigh about a hundred and thirty pounds. As for height, I'd judge you to be right at five-ten. Eyes are blue, hair brown, and you've got a scatter of freckles runnin' across your nose and cheekbones like fly-specks on a window pane.

"Your whiskers are still mostly fuzz, and it'll be a year or two before you can grow a proper beard. You pack a silver-mounted Colt's revolver on your right hip, but you wear your holster too low for quick work. Your spurs are Mexican made with star rowels, and it looks like you'll be needin' a new pair of boots before fall."

Hawks turned to face me then, and his faded blue eyes were red rimmed but steady. "I could tell you more," he said, "but there ain't that much more *to* you. Anyway, supper's ready."

I tried to think of something to say in reply, but drawed a total blank. This Hawks bird had a knack for keeping me off balance, and I can't say I was happy about it. He forked a steak onto each of three plates and dished up beans and taters from a pot at the back of the stove. He handed a plate to me, gave Ridgeway his, and set down on the woodbox. I finally found my tongue and told the man I was much obliged, then hunkered down by the stove, and we fell to eating. At least *some* people's mamas raised them with manners.

72

Nobody did much talking during supper, not even me. Now I like to talk and I like to eat, but it's hard to do either one well if you're trying to do them both at the same time. At least, that's my notion.

I will say Hawks cooked them steaks to a turn. I wolfed mine down and cleaned up the beans and taters he'd offered, and I saw that Marshal Ridgeway had done the same. When we'd finished, Hawks flung the bones outside to his hound, poured us each a cup of coffee, and led us out to a grassy patch east of the cabin. Of course, he brought his jug along, too. Once we settled ourselves on the grass, Ridgeway asked Hawks about his injury. "Couldn't help noticing that sling you're wearing," the marshal said. "What happened, if you don't mind my asking?"

Hawks took a pull on the jug and shrugged. "Bronc I was workin' bucked me off and walked on me some," he said. "Broke my arm just above the elbow."

Ridgeway looked over at the corral where the sorrel and the paint horse stood. "One of those two did that?" he asked.

Hawks shook his head. "No," he said, "another'n. Crazy, good for nothin' churn-head. I got rid of the som'bitch."

"Sold him, did you?"

"*Killed* him, by god. We been eatin' on him, dog and me. You boys have, too—we just had him for supper."

Ridgeway never turned a hair. "I believe that's

some of the best horse I've et," he said. "Merlin and me are obliged."

I felt like telling the marshal to speak for himself. I've never been all that particular about vittles, but I have generally drawed the line at eating my transportation. I hoped Hawks was joshing us, but I couldn't be sure. I took a half hitch on my tongue and tried to think about something else.

Ridgeway took out his tobacco pouch, filled his briar, and lit up. When he had the pipe going well, he squinted through the smoke at Hawks and said, "Reason I asked about your injury is I have a job for you, but I'm thinking your bad arm might hold you back."

Hawks nodded. "What *kind* of job?"

"Kind you do best," Ridgeway said. "Tracking. Tracking men. Vince and Cletus Coldwater kidnapped Thane McAllister's daughter last week. Thane went to pay the ransom, but he brought a couple of his men with him and the Coldwaters took offense.

"I expect the kidnappers will come back at Thane again. When they do, I want a deputy marshal and the best tracker in the territory—which would be you—on their trail."

Hawks looked thoughtful. "Speakin' of money, how much does this here job pay?"

"Two dollars a day and expenses while you're on the job. Bring the girl back safe and McAllister will pay you each a thousand more."

Hawks didn't say yes, but he didn't say no, either. For a time he just looked at Ridgeway, his eyes narrowed and a slight smile on his face. He helped himself to another drink, corked the jug, and set it beside him in the grass. Then he shifted his gaze to me. "And I suppose," he told Ridgeway, "part of the job is takin' care of the kid here. No thanks, Chance. I ain't runnin' no kidney-garden."

I saw red and only part of it was Hawks's nose. "I've got my own idea as to who would be taking care of who in such a pair-up, and *I* ain't interested either," I said. "I've got better things to do than play nursemaid to a burned out, one-armed drunk."

Because I had ofttimes in the past spoke myself into trouble, I made sure my gun hand was clear and my paunch was out of reach of the man's Bowie, but his attack never came. Hawks pulled the cork, tilted the jug up, and had himself another drink. He belched decorously, and wiped his mouth on his sleeve. Ridgeway seemed unperturbed. He drawed deep on his briar, sighed out a cloud of blue smoke, and spoke with calm and authority. "I didn't haul my tired old bones out into these badlands to watch you boys play Tomcats in the Moonlight," he said, "and you'll have to excuse me if I'm runnin' short on patience.

"Julie McAllister is out yonder somewheres in the hands of two of the most depraved desperados ever to hit this territory. She's no doubt tired, hurting, and scared half to death, poor thing, and *she's* the one *I'm* thinking about. Any day now, the Coldwater boys will make their move, and I want you two in place when that happens.

"Now you boys *will* work together, and that's an end to it. Whether or not you get along is up to you, but you will do what I tell you." The marshal looked Hawks in his bloodshot eyes and said, "*You* will because you *owe* me, and because you're a man who remembers his obligations."

Then Ridgeway turned to me and fixed me with that hard, ice-blue gaze of his. "And *you* will because you took an oath before God Almighty, and because you serve at my pleasure."

Ridgeway knocked the dottle out of his pipe and put the briar in his pocket. He looked just plain disgusted with us both. "So if you two knot-heads are going to fight," he said, "go ahead—get it out of your systems."

I couldn't look Ridgeway in the eye, so I just stared at the ground and felt ashamed of myself. "I ain't about to fight no one-armed old drunk," I muttered. "Wouldn't be right." Hawks scowled. "And I ain't fightin' no wet behind the ears schoolboy," he said. "Wouldn't want to make him cry."

"Then shake hands and behave yourselves," the marshal ordered, and we did.

I don't know whether it was the chitter of birdsong or the changing light that woke me, but I was up before dawn the next morning, feeling rested and ready to meet the day. The blue-haired hound shambled over when he saw I was awake, grinning from ear to ear the way hounds do and wagging his tail as though he thought I was his long-lost friend. He followed me over to the spring and watched with some interest as I washed up in its cold waters, but a passing jackrabbit caught his attention and I lost my audience.

I looked in at the cabin door and saw that both Ridgeway and Hawks were still asleep in their blankets. The marshal had made his bed on the floor beside the stove, while Hawks lay sprawled on a rude bunk against the wall. He lay on his back, dead to the world. A strangled snore rose from his open mouth and gave the birdsong ugly competition. His whiskey jug was on the floor beside his bed, near at hand.

I will admit I had my doubts about working with the man. Hawks had made it more than clear he didn't like me much, and I had not been all that impressed with him, either. But Ridgeway had put us in double harness, so I resolved to make the best of the situation.

I had put our horses in Hawks's corral the night before, and I sauntered on down and said good morning to Rutherford and the other ponies. In a nearby lean-to I found halters and lead ropes and took all four horses up to the spring for water. When they were finished drinking, I brought them back to the corral and poured out a scoopful of oats for each of them. Then I took currycomb and brush from the lean-to and gave them all a good grooming while they et. If there's anything more pleasant than the sound of horses eating oats in the cool of a morning, I don't know what it is.

By the time I got back to the cabin, woodsmoke was drifting up from the stovepipe. I knew Hawks was awake and fixing breakfast. I hoped he wasn't cooking horse again. The smell of coffee brewing took me by the nose and drawed me to the cabin door, but just as I was about to go in Marshal Ridgeway came out. He looked rumpled and grouchy as a wet owl and it didn't take a mind reader to know he'd slept poorly.

"Good mornin,' Marshal," I said.

Ridgeway snorted. "Don't 'good mornin' me," he said. "Any fool can see it's mornin', and *I'll* be the judge of how good it is."

Eyes narrowed to slits, the marshal stared off into the distance. "Take my advice, Merlin," he said. "Don't ever grow old. But if by some mischance you do, don't sleep on the rocky ground or the cold, hard floor of a badlands cabin. Roughing it tends to lose its appeal when a man reaches his golden years."

Breakfast was pretty much a repeat of the evening meal, including the mustang meat. The thought of eating horse still bothered me some, but I was bound not to let my feelings show. Besides, even though I hated to admit it, Hoodoo Hawks was a pretty good cook. My misgivings about being paired with the man were eased some when I realized we might have something in common after all. He was a good cook, and I was a champion eater.

After chuck, we cleaned up the dishes and helped Hawks close up his cabin. We put a pack outfit together and threw a diamond hitch on the sorrel, after which I saddled Hoodoo's paint, Ridgeway's Morgan, and my buckskin.

Then, just before we started out, Hawks caught up the blue-haired hound and tied him to a pine tree with a length of rope.

"You're not leaving that dog tied up, are you?" Ridgeway asked. "There's no telling how long it'll be before you get back."

Hawks shrugged. "He'll try to follow us if I don't tie him," he said. "I just want to keep him here 'til we get a mile or two down the trail."

"Well, who's going to turn him loose?"

"Oh, he'll turn *himself* loose, I reckon. Inside a half hour he'll chaw his way through that rope and be free. He'll be fine—I've left him alone before."

Ridgeway was becoming exasperated. "But when he gets loose, won't he come after us?"

"No," Hawks said patiently. "By the time he gets loose he'll have forgot why he *wanted* to. He'll rustle around, catch rabbits and such, and lay about the place 'til I get back."

Ridgeway tried one last time. "But damn it, man— you may be gone for weeks! Won't he quit you and run off?"

"Never has. Dog don't know what time it is.

Whether I come back tomorow or three months from now, it's pretty much the same to him. He'll be fine."

Ridgeway made no further response, but rolled his eyes heavenward and spurred the Morgan out on the trail to Dry Creek. Hawks fell in behind him on his paint, and I brought up the rear, leading the pack-horse. The blue-haired hound barked twice, then shifted into a mournful howl that would have done a timber wolf proud.

It was the near side of noon when we turned our horses onto Dry Creek's main street. The morning had gone from cool to passing hot, and the town slept beneath the summer sun like a turtle on a rock. Horses drowsed at the hitchrack in front of the Oasis Saloon, only their tails moving as they switched away the bluebottles and the horseflies. Heatwaves danced and shimmered in the flat light, and two town dogs sprawled in the shade of the big cottonwoods that flanked the Dry Creek Mercantile across the street.

I saw Hoodoo cast a longing eye toward the front door of the Oasis as we rode past, and for once I agreed with him. I had sweated through my shirt, my mouth was cotton dry, and the smell of Boogles's ice-cold beer came wafting out onto the street and invited us inside. I cleared my throat and was about to ask Marshal Ridgeway could we accept the invite when he turned in the saddle, shook his head, and said, "Later, boys. First, we need to call on Glenn Murdoch."

Glenn must have seen us coming. He was standing on the boardwalk in front of his office when we rode up, and his greeting was short and to the point. "You saved me a ride," he said. "I was about to come looking for you."

Ridgeway drew rein and read Glenn's face. He said nothing, but sat his horse and waited for Glenn to say the rest of it.

"Thane McAllister was just in here with Waco Calhoun," Glenn said. "He's heard from the Coldwaters again."

"And?"

"They sent him a lock of Julie's hair and asked him for another ten thousand."

six

The Cattleman's Bank of Dry Creek was the only brick building in town, and it stood four square and solid at the corner of Trail Street and Main. The top floor was occupied by the offices of a painless dentist and a threadbare lawyer, while on the first floor banker J. Wellington Sheets and a four-eyed teller named Dingle ran the bank for Thane McAllister. Thane had built the bank for his own convenience and to be close to his money, I suppose. Anyway, that's where we found him that day, coming out the door wearing a sour expression and carrying a leather satchel.

Thane had left Waco Calhoun out in front with the horses, and Waco caught his eye and nodded toward Ridgeway, Hoodoo, and me as we rode up. The big cowman took us in with a glance and looked up at Ridgeway. "You heard?" he asked.

"Yes," Ridgeway said, "Glenn told us."

Thane looked careworn. He gave Ridgeway a rueful smile and shrugged. "Well," he said. "You were right, Chance. You told me I'd hear from those sons o' bitches again and I did. Last night."

"And they demanded more money." It wasn't a question.

Thane's grin turned ghastly. "Now they want *another* ten thousand."

Ridgeway nodded. "Why don't we go over to the hotel and talk about this in private? No point in letting the whole town know our business."

"You're right again," Thane allowed. "Let's go."

Ridgeway stepped down and tied his horse to the bank's hitchrail. Hoodoo and me did likewise. Thane turned to Waco Calhoun and said, "Wait for me here, Waco. I'll be back directly." Then, turning on his heel, he led the way across the street.

The Grand Hotel of Dry Creek was neither grand nor much of a hotel, but it was a place a traveler could put up for a night, or a week if he wasn't too particular. A whitewashed two-story building just across Trail Street from the bank, the hotel boasted twelve rooms upstairs and a vestibule and dining room downstairs. A long veranda off the top floor shaded the front of the building, and double doors opened onto a spacious lobby that featured dusty furniture, potted palms, and the mounted heads and horns of several glass-eyed critters.

The desk clerk laid down his copy of the *Police Gazette* and smoothed back his hair when we came in, but when he saw we weren't there to rent a room, he shrugged and went back to his reading. Ridgeway led us to some overstuffed chairs near the front windows, and the four of us set down. "First off," Ridgeway told Thane, "I don't believe you've met Hoodoo Hawks. Hawks—say hello to Thane McAllister."

Thane didn't offer his hand. "I've heard of you," he told Hawks. "I understand you're a pretty fair tracker, when you're sober."

"I'm the best there is, drunk *or* sober," Hawks replied, "and I've heard of you, too. You're some kind of two-bit cow man, ain't you?"

Thane ignored the insult. "Yes," he said. "Some kind."

For maybe the twentieth time since I met Hawks I wondered how I'd ever be able to get along with him. Talking to the man seemed more like fighting a duel than conversation.

Ridgeway ignored him, too. He leaned toward Thane and got down to the subject at hand. "So," he said, "you've heard from the Coldwater boys again."

Thane produced a folded piece of paper from his shirt pocket. "Last evenin'," he said, "around sundown. Waco found this note and a ring tacked to the ranch gate with a horseshoe nail."

Ridgeway put on his spectacles, cleared his throat, and unfolded the note. At the center of the paper a silver ring with a turquoise stone caught sunlight. Gently, the marshal picked up the ring and held it in his left hand. "Julie's?" he asked. Thane's face was drawn, his voice tight with anger. He looked at Ridgeway and nodded.

The marshal unfolded the paper. Slowly, and in a calm tone of voice, he read the note aloud.

MCALLISTER—
WE'RE RAISING THE STAKES! DELIVER ANOTHER
$10,000 TO ALKALI SPRINGS SUNUP WENSDY OR WE
KIL YUR DAUTER. NO LAWDOGS!
WE MEAN BISNESS!
SINED BY HAND   VINCE & CLETUS COLDWATER

Carefully, Ridgeway folded the note again, removed his spectacles, and put them away inside his vest. "I hate to speak ill of the feeble-minded," he said, "but them Coldwater boys are dumb as rocks. Not only have they sent you two separate ransom notes, they've *signed* this one—in their own hand!"

"They may be dumb," Thane said, "but they're about to wind up with a total of twenty thousand dollars of my money. If them boys get any dumber I may have to sell the ranch.

"The point is," he continued, "they've got my

Julie! I'd like to skin them bastards alive and stake 'em out on an ant pile, but I can't—not until Julie's safe at home." He had placed the satchel on the floor by his chair; now he reached down and patted the bag with his hand. "So I'll take them their damn money. Does anybody know where this Alkali Springs place is?"

Remembering, Ridgeway glanced at me and nodded. Two years previous, the marshal and me had been part of a showdown there that neither of us would ever forget. Oh, I knew where Alkali Springs was, all right.

"I know it well," I said. "It's south of here, maybe fifteen miles east of Brimstone Gap. Used to be a dry-land spread, but it's been abandoned for years. Nothing there now but an old cabin, fallen in on itself, and a weed-grown barn."

Ridgeway nodded. "I can see why the Coldwaters picked the place," he said. "From the top of that mesa above the barn, a man can see five miles in every direction."

The marshal looked thoughtful. "This second note said nothing about you coming alone," he told Thane. "In fact, it didn't say you had to come at all. I think it might be safer if you didn't."

Thane jumped to his feet. The lobby shook like an earthquake had hit it. "I have to pay them!" he said. "I'm not calling their bluff with Julie's life at stake!"

"I didn't say you shouldn't *pay* them," Ridgeway said. "I said it might be best if you didn't go there *yourself.* Those boys might just kill you and keep Julie *and* the money."

"You paint a hell of a picture. What else can I do?"

Ridgeway nodded at me. "What if we send young Merlin in with the money? He knows Alkali Springs and he knows your daughter. If everything goes well, he'll be back here with her tomorrow night."

"And if everything *don't* go well?"

"Hoodoo goes with him. Camps maybe three miles from Alkali Springs. Merlin goes on ahead, meets the Coldwaters, and gives them the money. If anything goes wrong with the trade, Merlin and Hoodoo are already in position to deal with the situation, whatever it is."

"What about the part of the note that says 'no lawdogs'?"

"Well, it ain't like Merlin will be wearing his *badge*. He'll tell them he's one of your cowboys. Which he was."

"What if they take the money and kill Merlin?"

Ridgeway stroked his moustache. When he spoke, his voice was somber, but there was a twinkle in his eye. "Why, I suppose that's just a chance I'll have to *take*," he said.

Which is how Hoodoo Hawks and me came to be riding out of Dry Creek at one o'clock of a Tuesday afternoon without so much as a glass of beer to fortify us on our journey. Marshal Ridgeway gave me three one hundred dollar bank notes to use as traveling money, and made me sign for it, of course. He said a man could never tell what he would encounter on the trail, and that he never liked to send a deputy out without some cash in his pocket. He also said I could buy supplies and such with a promissory note drawn on Uncle Sam, or even requisition supplies if need be. To tell the truth, I never paid much attention to his instructions at the time. I told myself that all I had to do was deliver the ransom money and bring Julie back. I did wrap the hundred-dollar notes around a wad of dollar bills. and stuffed the money in my pocket along with a handful of coins.

Ridgeway took a room at the hotel and told me he'd stay in town until the following evening when we'd be back with Julie. Thane McAllister had his misgivings, I could tell, but he bowed to Ridgeway's judgment. McAllister looked all of his three hundred and some pounds as he handed me the satchel and said, "I don't care a damn about the money, but don't you let anything happen to my little girl. *You hear me?*"

I allowed as how I heard him, all right, and swore that I would stop at nothing to protect Julie, which was the plain truth.

I confess I was surprised at how well Hoodoo took our not being able to visit the saloon. Two miles from town I was leading the sorrel packhorse down a narrow trail with Hoodoo behind me on his paint when I looked back to see how the pack was riding. And there was Hoodoo, whiskey bottle tipped up toward the sun, his adam's apple bobbing as he swallered.

"Hey!" I yelled.

The tracker was all innocence. He held the bottle out to me and grinned. "Want some?" he asked.

"No, I don't," I told him, "and you shouldn't be a-drinkin' that nose paint, either! We've got serious work to do, and whiskey ain't part of the deal."

"*You* have serious work ahead, not me," Hoodoo said. "All I have to do is camp three miles from Alkali Springs and wait 'til you come back with the cowman's kid. How hard can *that* be?"

If I'd had doubts before, now they were multiplying like rabbits. What Hoodoo said was true, and I knew I couldn't make him quit drinking without shooting him. In the end I didn't give up so much as I made a temporary truce. "Well," I said, "try not to fall off your dang horse."

The country south of Dry Creek grew hotter and drier by the mile. We rode through sun-blasted gullies and washouts, across low and broken buttes and dry creek beds. Off to the west, in the distance, the cool mass of the Brimstone Mountains reared up against the sky like a great blue island, and the only sounds were the wind and the sometime clatter of a horse's hoof scraping rock.

Behind me, Hoodoo brought up the rear of our two-man posse in silence, which was more than all right with me. I have already mentioned that trying to have a conversation with the man was more work than pleasure, and I took advantage of the quiet to make my plans. It had been just over two years since I'd last been to Alkali Springs, but the memory stood out sharp and clear, and I recalled the region as if I was already there.

First, there was the lone butte that towered above the ramshackle barn and cabin. Beyond, sparse dry grass waved in the wind out on the flat and along the jumbled coulees. Then there was the low basin of the spring itself, alkali white as snow along its edges. Beyond the basin stood the gray green greasewood patch, thick and jumbled, some of it tall as a man.

The sun dropped low above the mountains, and the long shadows of early evening reached out like fingers holding on to the light. Below us, a narrow creek twisted over the valley's broken floor, and a raggle-taggle stand of cottonwoods huddled at the water's edge. Off in the distance, I saw with my eyes what I had just seen in memory—the flat-topped butte above Alkali Springs, ablaze in the late light. I drew rein and turned in my saddle.

Hoodoo was still with me, after a fashion. He swayed unsteadily atop his paint horse and grinned, his cheeks flushed and his nose red. The pint bottle was nowhere in sight, but its effects were clear. I pointed to the cottonwood grove. "We'll make camp there," I told him. "There's water aplenty and grass for the horses. There's wood, too, but we won't be needing a fire tonight." I looked out across the valley.

"That butte yonder is just above the springs. A man watching from up there could see a fire from a long way off."

Hoodoo caught the saddle horn with his good hand and slid off the paint. "Then it's cold beans and jerked beef for supper," he said. "How far do you figure it is to the springs?"

I stepped off Rutherford and looked at the butte. Only the very top still caught light. "I'd say just over three miles," I told him.

"More like five," Hoodoo said. "I just wondered how good you are at figuring distance. Evidently, you ain't. Good at it, I mean."

I was in no mood for argument so I let the remark pass. I have never enjoyed personal criticism, especially when it's true. I loosened the cinch on my saddle, hobbled Rutherford, and slipped off the bridle so he could graze. Then I turned my attentions to the packhorse and relieved it of its burden.

By the time I'd rolled out my bed beside the creek and had set out the rawhide panniers containing our grub and possibles, the sun had slid behind the mountains and lit the clouds on fire. Deep shadows softened the harshness of the badlands, and a cool breeze came drifting down the creek and promised relief from the day's heat.

Before leaving Dry Creek I had transferred the ransom money from Thane's satchel to my saddlebags. Now, in the clearing by the creek, I checked the bags again. The money was still there, of course; five bundles, each bundle containing forty fifty-dollar bank notes. Carefully, I rebuckled the flaps on the bags and tried to shake off the edgy feeling that had commenced to come over me. I looked toward the mesa that marked my coming meeting with the Cold-water boys and took a deep breath.

"That flat-topped butte is still out there, kid," Hoodoo said, "and the money is still in your saddlebags. All that's left to do now is make the trade and get the girl back." There was a brief pause, then he spoke again, softer than before. "I expect you'll do fine," he said.

His words surprised me. Gone was the quarrelsome, feisty tone he had used on me since the day we met. I turned and looked into his eyes. They were red rimmed, but friendly. "Well," he said, rummaging through the panniers, "I'm ready for some of that jerky and them cold beans. How about you?"

"I was born ready," I told him.

Hoodoo and me didn't talk much that evening. We ate our cold supper by the creek and tended the horses. Then, for a time we just sat and listened to the night. The creek rippled over its rocky bed and reflected light back at the sky. Somewhere upstream a bullfrog croaked his solemn music. Far out in the breaks a bur-rowing owl sang his *coo-hoo* like a man blowing into a jug. The evening star came out and so did the skeeters, rising up from the grass along the creek. Skeeters seldom bother me much, but that night I found their high-pitched whine irritating as finger-nails on a slate. I kept waiting for them to light on me, which somewhat derailed my train of thought.

The sky was still light when I turned in and pulled the canvas tarp of my bedroll up over my face. As I laid there in my blankets I went over the layout at Alkali Springs again in my mind. I saw in memory the tumbled-down cabin, the sun-bleached barn, and the white-rimmed springs. Who would be there to meet me? The Coldwater boys, maybe others. And Julie, pretty Julie. Scared, for sure. Hurt, maybe. She'd be glad to see me and grateful to her daddy for buying her freedom.

I have to do this right, I thought. I would leave before first light and be waiting at the barn at sunup. I would take no weapon, give the kidnappers no trouble. I would bring them their money, keep a tight rein on my smart mouth and my temper, and do whatever they told me. Time enough to hunt them down when Julie is safe. Plenty of time then for the law and justice. After a time my eyelids commenced to grow heavy, and I fell asleep to the drone of skeeters and the memory of Julie McAllister's sweet smile.

When next I woke the Dipper sat level just above the horizon, so I reckoned the time to be just about four in the morning. The land still slept, dark and silent under a starry sky, with nary a breath of wind. Hoodoo was already up, and he bade me good day with a mutter. "If you don't like cold beans and whiskey," he said, "breakfast is over."

"Crick water will do me fine," I told him. "I know it don't sound much like me, but I really don't believe I could eat a *bite* this morning."

"Nerves," Hoodoo said. "Appetite shuts down when the mind's workin' overtime."

I saddled Rutherford and led him to the creek for water while Hoodoo looked on. "If everything goes right, I should be back here with Julie in an hour or so," I said. The moment I heard myself say "if everything goes right" I was sorry. Somehow it sounded like I was worried, like I feared things might *not* go right, but Hoodoo either hadn't heard me or chose not to comment.

I gave Hoodoo my badge and six-gun, buckled on my shaps, and swung up on Rutherford. "Well," I said, "I'll see you directly."

I expect it was in Hoodoo's mind—I know it was in mine—but neither of us added, "if everything goes right."

The badlands came awake slowly as I rode, full dark giving way to shades of gray. Rutherford stepped out smartly, weaving his way through the sage and greasewood in a go-to-work, clear-footed trot. From time to time the buckskin broke the rhythm of his gait. I would feel him pause in his dogtrot, then bunch and gather himself to clear some obstacle I could not yet see.

Over east, a thin line of red bloodied the sky, and I

began to make out some detail within the gloom. The heavens growed lighter. Off to my left, sunlight painted the peaks of the Brimstones and chased the stars away. I would reach Alkali Springs in plenty of time. Straight ahead, the flat-topped butte bulked heavy and dark against cloudless skies.

Sunlight exploded through the notch that was Brimstone Gap and sent long rays of brightness across the badlands. Rutherford whuffed, grunting, as he stepped off into a shadowed wash, then gathered himself and lunged back up and out into the daylight. I slowed the buckskin from a trot to a walk as I rounded the mesa's base. The weathered old barn, looking lonesome and forlorn, came into view as I topped the rise. In the valley below, still in shadow, lay the abandoned cabin, weed-grown and fallen in upon itself. The old windmill stood on spindly legs above the springs, the rotting blades of its fan wheel like the petals of a dead sunflower.

I drew rein and pulled the buckskin to a stop. Barely breathing, I sat, listening. Rutherford bowed his neck, rubbing the side of his head against his foreleg, and I heard the clicking of his bridle bit, loud in the stillness. Beyond the barn, a raven rode the rising air currents out across the valley, its call raucous and rude. I shifted in the saddle, and heard the leathers creak. I held my breath. Tense as a bowstring, I waited.

It was Rutherford who let me know we weren't alone. A low nicker rumbled deep in his throat, and he raised his head, tasting the air. His ears pointed back at a sound I couldn't hear. A bead of sweat crept out from beneath my hat brim and crawled down past my ear. The voice that broke the stillness came from behind me, harsh, and ugly as a bruise. "Step down off that goddam horse," it said. "Keep your hands high and your eyes on the ground. Make any *other* move, and you'll be a long time dead."

seven

I did as I was told. Slow and careful, I slid out of the saddle and stepped away from Rutherford. Hands high, I waited for whatever would come next.

"All right," rasped the voice, "you can turn around."

I kept my hands high. Turning slowly, I found myself facing a man of about my height and weight. He was dressed from hat to boots in dusty black, and his face was covered to the eyes by a black silk bandanna. I tried to ignore the Winchester rifle the man held trained on my middle, but without success. I felt someone step close and pat me down, searching for weapons, I supposed.

"He ain't heeled, Vince," said a man's voice from behind me.

The gent with the rifle seemed to study me for a long minute. When at last he spoke, his voice had a husky sound, as though his throat hurt. "Where's

Thane McAllister, and who the hell are you?" he asked.

"Thane sent me," I said. "I'm Merlin Fanshaw. I ride for the M-Cross."

"The hell you say. Why didn't the old he-bull come himself?"

"He's feelin' poorly. Anyway, the note never said he had to. It said he was to *deliver* the money here at sunup today."

"I know what the goddam note said," the man said. "I *wrote* the goddam note. You bring the money?"

"Ten thousand in bank notes. The money's in my saddlebags."

The man with the rifle shifted his glance to a point behind me. "Is it all there, Clete?" he asked.

From the corner of my eye I caught sight of a second man—the one who'd patted me down, I figured. He was standing beside my Rutherford horse, and he held my saddlebags before him. He, too, was dressed in black and masked, same as the man who'd braced me. Quickly, he pawed through the bundled bank notes. "Appears to be," he said.

The man with the rifle turned his attentions back to me. "All right, cowboy," he said, "you've made your delivery. You can go now."

"Uh . . . what about McAllister's daughter? What about the girl?"

"What *about* her?"

"I brought the money, like you said to. I'm supposed to take her back with me."

"I believe we'll just keep her a while longer, until we put some distance between us and the law."

I could feel the anger building inside me, like steam in a boiler. I set my jaw and shook my head. "That ain't right," I told him. "You said in your note you'd turn her loose."

"Like hell I did. The note said bring the money or we'd *kill* her. Didn't say nothin' about turnin' her loose."

I tried to keep a cool head. I really did. I tried to stay calm and steady, the way I imagined Marshal Ridgeway would, but it was a losing cause. I kept thinking about Julie, scared and lonesome, maybe abused by these men, and I could feel my anger turn to rage.

"I ain't leavin' here without her," I said. My voice sounded like a rasp scraping metal. The rifleman took a step backward and brought the Winchester to bear again. "Your choice, cowboy," he said. "You may not be leavin' here at all."

Looking back on it now, I really believe I had lost control of myself enough to try to take on the man with my bare hands. I took a step toward him. That's when I heard Julie's voice. I heard her cry out from somewhere behind me, "Don't, Merlin! He'll kill you!"

I turned my head, saw Julie inside the barn's doorway. Her dark eyes were open wide, sleek black hair framing her face. I stared open-mouthed, then turned back to the rifleman again. Whatever chance I might have had was gone, lost in the moment of Julie's shout. The man stepped in close, swung the rifle up, and I felt the butt smash into my jaw. White light exploded behind my eyes and went to red. I told my legs to take me to the man, but they refused. I felt myself falling, the world a crimson blur going to black. The earth rose up to greet me, but I do not recall the moment of our meeting.

Now if you've never been knocked unconscious, you might think from reading wild West adventures and such that the experience is something like a sudden, unintended nap. The hero of them dime novels generally comes back to his senses full of fight and ready to ride out after the villain who slugged him, and we all shout hurrah at his spunk. Well, I have to tell you that ain't at all the way it really is. I have been struck senseless on more than one occasion, and I have found the experience to be one that few people would care to repeat.

I have no idea how long I laid there with my face in the dirt, but I came to with a hurting in my head and body that went well beyond mere pain. I opened my eyes a crack, but the brightness caused me to repent of my folly and I squinched them shut again. My jaw throbbed, my tongue felt big as a cow's, and my mouth was dry as alkali dust. I had some trouble collecting my thoughts, and I felt a powerful urge to throw up the contents of my paunch.

"You just going to lay there, are you?"

I rolled over and sat up, facing the sound of the voice. Bright splinters of light exploded through my brain, and a sharp, stabbing pain clawed like a trapped cat behind my eyes. "Who—who are you?" I inquired.

"It's your faithful pardner," said the voice, "come to rouse you from your slumbers."

I opened one eye a crack, then the other. Hoodoo Hawks stood, looking down at me, the sun at his back. Behind him, his paint horse and the sorrel pack-horse switched flies in the sunshine. "Go to hell," I said.

Hawks took a pint bottle from his buckskin coat and pulled the cork.

Whiskey fumes polluted the morning air. He handed the bottle to me. "I expect to, sooner or later," he said pleasantly, "but not just yet."

I took a long swig from the flask, hoping the whiskey would help restore me to my senses. What it did was push my troubled innards over the edge. I hunkered down behind a clump of greasewood and heaved up everything my stomach contained. I can't be sure, but I think some of my internal organs may have come up as well. After I completed that performance I found with some surprise that I *did* feel better. The hurt seemed to ease up a bit, and a little of my old spunk returned. "I thought you were going to wait for me back where we camped," I said. "Comin' here could have messed up my meeting."

"Seems like *you* done that already," Hawks replied.

"I didn't leave camp until I saw them boys through the long glass, ridin' west. Two men and a girl, they was. And, I suppose, the ransom money."

"Yeah."

I stood up, slow and careful, and took a firm grip on the earth with my toes. When the world stopped spinning some, I opened my eyes and looked around. Thirty yards downhill from the barn the kidnappers had tied Rutherford to a sagebrush. The buckskin sniffed the air and whinnied, pawing up dust with a front foot. Well, I thought, at least the bastards didn't steal my horse.

When I turned my attention back to Hoodoo, I saw he was bent over at the waist, studying the ground. I don't know what all he was seeing, but he looked like a man reading a good book. "If you're studying their tracks," I said, "you're wastin' your time. You just told me you saw them riding west."

"Readin' tracks is never a waste of time, kid," Hawks said. "You want to tell me what happened?"

"Coldwater boys took the money, but wouldn't give up the girl. I made a fuss and got clubbed with a rifle butt."

"You saw the girl?"

"I did. She called me by name, just before Vince Coldwater put me down."

"How'd you know it was Vince Coldwater?"

"His brother Clete called *him* by name. And before you ask, I know it was Cletus Coldwater because Vince called *him* by name. You got any *more* questions?"

Hoodoo still carried his left arm in the black silk bandanna that served as a sling, but he took my gun belt from the forks of his saddle with his good hand and gave it to me. "No questions," he said, "but I have a few observations. First off, I don't believe you were dealin' with the Coldwater boys."

"Somethin' wrong with your hearing? I just *told* you they called each other by name!"

Hoodoo took another pull at the whiskey flask and emptied it. "Yes, you did," he allowed, "but I met the Coldwater boys two years ago up in Miles City. Didn't get to know them well, but I learned a few things."

I buckled my gun belt about my waist. Hoodoo Hawks had a positive knack for raising my hackles. "Like what?" I asked.

"Like—Vince and Clete Coldwater both have about the biggest feet I ever saw on a man—size fourteen or better. Tracks here in the dirt ain't but size nine or ten."

"What are you saying?"

"I'm sayin' we may be dealing with kidnappers, all right, but whoever they are, they *ain't* the Coldwater boys."

Hoodoo's words hung in the air like smoke after a pistol shot. I don't know if it was getting my bell rung like I had or if I had suddenly gone slow of wit, but I was having trouble getting my mind around his news. I untied Rutherford from the bush and laid my face against his neck. "Well," I said, "if they ain't the Coldwaters, who are they?"

Hoodoo swung into his saddle and pointed his pony due west. "Damn if I know. Somebody who wants their crime *blamed* on the Coldwaters, maybe. I'm a tracker, not a fortune teller. What I do know is we need to get on their trail before we all perish of old age. You comin'?"

I spurred Rutherford out ahead of Hoodoo's pony. "Hell yes, I'm coming," I told him. "I'm the *leader* of this outfit."

We took to the ridges, following the kidnappers' tracks as they led out through the greasewood and sage. I held Rutherford to a fast, ground-covering trot, with Hoodoo and the packhorse following, and we rode the dry and broken country south of Alkali Springs at a lively clip. My head still hurt and my back teeth felt loose, but I did feel some improved, even if I was baffled by the turn of events. Back in Dry Creek, Marshal Ridgeway would be waiting. Come evening, Thane McAllister would be expecting us to return with his daughter Julie, unharmed and redeemed by the ransom he'd paid. I knew it was my duty to let Ridgeway know what had happened, but I also knew that going back to Dry Creek could mean losing the kidnappers' trail, and maybe Julie.

By midafternoon it became clear that we weren't narrowing the gap much between the outlaws and ourselves. Each time Hoodoo and me reached the top of a ridge I'd expect to see Julie and the two men off in the distance, but I never did. Finally, at the top of a long, steep hill just beyond the railroad tracks that led to Silver City, I drew rein and waited for Hoodoo to catch up. Directly, he came clattering up on his paint pony with the packhorse in tow, and drew rein alongside me. Both his horse and mine were lathered and breathing hard. I stepped down and loosened my cinch. Hoodoo shook his head. "They're better mounted than us." he said. "We ain't a-going to run them down."

"Just what I was thinking," I said. "When you saw them this morning through the long glass, could you tell what kind of horses they were riding?"

"Big horses," Hoodoo said. "Thoroughbreds, most likely. A bay and a chestnut. Girl was ridin' a black."

"There's a cavalry post about six miles west of here," I said. "Fort Savage. I can telegraph Ridgeway from there, let him know what happened back at the Springs. Maybe I can requisition some fresh horses, too."

"And then?"

"Then we pick up the kidnappers' trail again, while we still have some daylight. You up to that, tracker?"

Hoodoo shrugged. "It's your girl hunt. I'm only the hired help. Anything else?"

"Yes, one thing," I said. "I'm putting my *badge* back on."

The country changed as we neared Fort Savage. Badlands became grassy plains, and bare desert ridges gave way to rolling hills and buttes, topped by jack-pine and cedar. Hoping to make up lost time, I pushed my Rutherford horse some, alternating between a trot and a lope. Thirty yards behind me, Hoodoo brought the packhorse along and kept the pace. I figured he was still sizing me up, not being sure just what kind of pardner he had got himself teamed up with. I know I was still sizing *him* up.

I had plenty to think about. Marshal Ridgeway had trusted me to deliver the ransom money and fetch Julie back, but I had accomplished only the first half of that mission. I had delivered the money, all right, but the kidnappers still had Julie. Worse, I had lost my temper—after vowing I would not—and got myself knocked unconscious. I had a swollen jaw and a mean headache to remind me of my folly. All things considered, I was less than pleased with the way my first mission as a deputy U.S. marshal was going.

Who *were* the kidnappers? If they weren't the Coldwater boys, why had they claimed they were? Obviously, they wanted to conceal their identities. Maybe they also wanted folks to think they were a higher class of outlaw than they really were. I had read somewhere that in the heyday of the James gang the boys had been blamed for many a robbery that some want-to-be-famous outlaw gang really pulled off. Maybe, I thought, it was the same with the Coldwaters.

One thing I did know—I would neither falter nor turn back until I found Julie again and rescued her from her abductors. I would push ahead despite opposition, accident, or my whiskey drinking partner. I would get the job done. I would prevail, come hell, high water, or Coldwaters, for that matter. I would, I told myself, succeed in my mission no matter *how* bad things got.

Fort Savage had been built to protect railroad construction crews from hostile Indians, but incidents between the track layers and the Crow, who called that country home, turned out to be few and far between. Now and then some young bucks from the reservation would make off with a few of Uncle Sam's horses, and a patrol from the fort would ride out to fetch them back. The troopers would generally wander around until both they and their mounts were played out, and find nothing, of course. Then they would slink on back to the garrison and nurse their saddle sores. I felt sorry for the soldiers. Troopers at Fort Savage found themselves with little to do except listen to the wind blow and drink whiskey, so that's mostly how they spent their time. Drinking helped take the edge off the boredom, but it tended to be hard on the liver.

Like most forts in the West, Fort Savage was not enclosed, but marked its boundaries by the lay of its buildings, corrals, and such. The rust-colored stream that trickled past the fort was aptly named Sidewinder Creek, for it twisted back and forth upon itself like a snake track.

Across the creek, a long adobe structure with a sod

roof sprawled within a ragged grove of cottonwood trees. It did not seem to be part of the fort's buildings, yet it was only a pistol shot away from them. As Hoodoo and me splashed across the creek I saw a bearded trooper glance our way before he ducked through a doorway and went inside.

Hoodoo rode up beside me. He grinned one of those just-between-us-boys grins and asked, "You know what that place is, don't you, deputy?"

"No," says I, "but from the look of joy on your face it probably has something to do with whiskey."

The grin got wider. "You're *part* right," Hoodoo said. "That there is a hog ranch."

I looked at the building. "I don't see no hogs."

Hoodoo's laugh was more cackle than laughter. "The hogs is inside the building," he chortled, "and they're mostly *female!* I swear, I thought *everybody* knowed what a hog ranch is!"

I did my best to save face. "Oh!" I said. "*That* kind of hog ranch. Of *course* I know what a hog ranch is. It's just that I have more important things on my mind right now than whores and whiskey."

"Leadership is a terrible burden," Hoodoo said.

Apparently, the young sentry hadn't challenged anyone for awhile. He looked to be about thirteen years old, and his voice broke right in the middle of "Halt! Who goes there?" as we approached the fort. When I showed him my badge and asked to see his commander he didn't seem to know whether to shoot

106

or salute. In the end, he solved his indecision the army way. He passed the problem on to someone else. "Corporal of the Guard!" he yelled. "Visitors to see the major!"

When the corporal showed up, I repeated my story. "I'm Merlin Fanshaw, Corporal," I told him. "Deputy U.S. Marshal on official business. I need to speak to your commanding officer."

"Sorry, sir," the corporal said. "Major Burdette is indisposed."

"What kind of indisposed?"

Now it was the corporal's turn to look indecisive. "He—uh—he's taking a bath—over at the bath house, sir."

"Could you let him know I'm here, Corporal? It's important."

"Yes, sir. Right away, sir. Follow me, sir—you can wait for the major at headquarters."

I dismounted and gave the corporal a friendly grin. "You don't need to 'sir' me unless you have a mind to," I said. "We both work for Uncle Sam, so I figure that makes us cousins."

The corporal wasn't taking any chances. "Yes, sir," he said.

Hoodoo allowed as how he had already seen all the army majors he cared to, so I left him to mind the horses while I followed the corporal across the parade ground to the headquarters building. The corporal took me into Major Burdette's office and showed me to a chair.

"Please be seated, sir," he said. "I'll tell the major you're here."

After the corporal had gone I took a look around. I expect the major's office was fairly typical for a frontier fort of the time. Log walls, freshly chinked, held photographs of Abraham Lincoln, U. S. Grant, and President Chester Arthur. A fly-specked calendar displayed the day of the month and year. A rusted Sibley stove stood in a box of sand, its stovepipe extending up and through the roof. Behind the major's desk, filing cabinets and the Stars and Stripes flanked a map of the territory. The major's belt, scabbard, and saber hung from a peg near the open door.

I stood up, looking out at the parade ground. Across the way, at the enlisted men's barracks, troopers were airing their bedding. Over near the stables a platoon marched together in close order drill. The day was sunny, with a mild breeze stirring the dust. I wondered where Julie was. I wondered *how* Julie was.

I found myself growing impatient. Every minute we stayed at the fort the kidnappers lengthened their lead. I longed to be back on their trail, pursuing them, narrowing the distance between us. I began to pace the floor. Where was the major? What was keeping him?

Just then he appeared at the door, the corporal beside him. The major was a short man, maybe five foot two, with deep-set eyes and a double chin.

His hair was still wet and his cheeks were ruddy from his bath. He extended his hand. "Major Edmund

Burdette," he said. "I've been known to pace that floor myself. How may I help you?"

I took his hand. "Merlin Fanshaw, out of Dry Creek. Chance Ridgeway's newest deputy."

Burdette eased himself into his swivel chair, his hands together atop his desk. He gave me a polite nod, waiting for me to continue.

"I'm here with a tracker, on the trail of two men and a woman," I told him. "We lost their trail a ways back."

"Too bad. Again, how may I be of help?"

"Two ways, Major. First. I need to telegraph Marshal Ridgeway and make a report. Is the line between here and Dry Creek still up?"

"You're in luck, Deputy. The line was down earlier in the week, but a patrol found the break and repaired it. You said *two* ways."

"The fugitives are better mounted than we are. We could use some fresh horses."

Burdette sighed. "Afraid I can't help you there, Deputy. We're more than fifty head short over the past few months. Lost, strayed, or—as I suspect—stolen. I can't prove it, but I believe the animals may have been—borrowed—by our neighbors, the Crow."

The major struck a pose. Standing, he clasped his hands behind his back and stared off through the door at the distant hills. When he spoke again, he seemed to be talking more to himself than to me. "This fort is beginning to look more like an *infantry* post than a *cavalry* command."

Burdette turned to me and grinned a rueful grin. "I'm sorry, deputy. You didn't come here to listen to *my* troubles. Let's go send your telegraph."

eight

The post telegrapher did double duty as company clerk. He was an old-line regular sergeant, and he snapped to attention like a first-year cadet when Major Burdette and me walked into the office.

"As you were, Sergeant," said the major. "Deputy Fanshaw here needs to send a telegraph to Dry Creek."

"Yes, sir," the sergeant replied, pushing a pad and pencil across the desk. "If the deputy will write out his message—"

"I pretty much know what I want to say," I told him. "The message is from me, Merlin Fanshaw. It goes to Chance Ridgeway, U.S. Marshal. He's staying at the Grand Hotel in Dry Creek."

The sergeant opened the key. "Whenever you're ready, Deputy," he said.

I thought a moment, trying to phrase the message so that only Ridgeway would savvy its meaning. "Send this," I said. "PAID FOR MERCHANDISE BUT SELLERS REFUSED TO DELIVER. AM ENROUTE TO COLLECT. WILL CONTACT YOU WHEN TRANSACTION COMPLETE." The sergeant tapped out the message as I spoke, then stopped. A moment later the key clattered briefly, then went silent.

"Message went through," the sergeant said. "That was the Dry Creek operator."

"Much obliged," I told him. Turning to Major Burdette, I said, "Reckon I'd best be moving on, Major. There's still a few good hours of daylight."

Burdette nodded. "You and your tracker are welcome to stay for evening mess. And to spend the night, if you wish."

"That's mighty temptin'," I told him, "but I hope to narrow the fugitives' lead. Another time."

The major looked thoughtful. "About those horses you need. There is a rancher named George Keppler, over on Curlew Creek, who has horses. His place is about nine miles due west of here. The man is something of a sharp trader, but he might help you."

"Much obliged, Major," I said. "I'll look him up."

The smell of roast beef came wafting across the parade ground from the mess hall as I passed and nearly caused me to change my mind about getting an early start. I had heard that army food tended toward the tasteless and skimpy, but I had never been what you could call particular. I figured grub was grub, when you got right down to it. Most days I was more concerned with filling my paunch than with the quality of the cooking. For a moment I gave thought to taking the major up on his invite. There was no reason we *couldn't* stay for supper, maybe spend the night, too. My jaw still throbbed from where it had met with the rifle butt, and I was feeling trail weary. It would be good to get some shut-eye before taking to the trail again. Be good to rest the horses, too. Hoodoo and me could be up and on our way early in the morning, even before the bugler blowed his horn.

Then I recalled Julie McAllister's face. I remembered the way she had looked that morning at Alkali Springs when she'd called out my name. She had looked so beautiful and defenseless it like to have broke my heart just to recall it. Julie was a prisoner of two hard men and in mortal danger, yet her concern had been for *my* safety! It was almost more than a man could credit. I knew right then I would not be eating roast beef at the mess hall nor spending the night at Fort Savage neither. Hoodoo and me would seek out and find the kidnappers' trail. We would foller and keep a-dogging them boys until we had Julie back with us, safe and sound.

I found the horses at the edge of the fort. Hoodoo had hobbled and left them to graze on the scant grass along Sidewinder Creek. The young sentry was no longer on guard duty, but he hadn't left the area. He turned his head when he heard me walk up, and grinned a boyish grin. "Howdy again, Deputy," he said.

"Howdy yourself," I said. "You don't happen to know where my tracker went, do you?"

The sentry's grin turned sly. He nodded toward the adobe building across the creek. "Yessir, I reckon I do," he said. "Seems like he had some urgent business yonder at the hog ranch."

"I might have knowed. Tell you what, son—I'm going to take our horses and ride over to that long hill west of here. When I get to the top, I'll let the ponies catch their breath and graze on the buffalo grass while I have me some jerked beef and admire the view."

I dug a silver dollar out of my pants pocket and handed it to the youngster. He took the coin, questions in his eyes.

"Now when you see me ride out on top, I'd like you to go find my tracker and tell him where I've gone. If he moves right along I'll wait for him. Shouldn't take him more than a half hour or so to walk it."

The sentry's eyebrows went up. He shook his head, the grin coming back. "He's gonna be awful mad," he said.

I answered his grin with one of my own. "Yes," I said, "I expect he will."

A wide, sloping plain led to the hills a half mile west of Fort Savage.

Leading the packhorse and Hoodoo's paint, I kicked Rutherford into a brisk trot and headed out. The wind had risen since the morning and now gusted out of the west, rippling the grass and singing through the sagebrush. I screwed my hat down tighter, lowered my head, and rode away toward the hill I'd pointed out to the sentry.

Rutherford had most of the traits I had admired in other buckskins. He never balked nor hung back, but responded wholehearted to rein and spur. He seemed to enjoy being under saddle and on the go, and it was no time at all until we reached the foothills. I tried to make it easy on the little horse and take him up the slope in a series of zigzags, but he would have none of it. Instead, he attacked the hill head-on, carrying me and leading the other horses on to the top.

At the summit, I stepped off the buckskin and tied all three horses to a scrub cedar before turning my attention to the valley below. I took Hoodoo's spy-glass from his saddlebag and focused it. The glass was a good one. Beyond the plain, the buildings of the fort stood out in sharp relief. I scanned the parade ground, saw the flag snapping smartly in the breeze. I found the headquarters building, the enlisted men's barracks, the stables, and the mess hall. I found the young sentry, saw him look my way, then turn and cross the footbridge over Sidewinder Creek. I sat cross-legged in the loose dirt and rock of the hilltop, rested my elbows on my knees, and watched as the young trooper entered the door to the hog ranch. I brought the glass into sharper focus, and waited.

Suddenly, the sentry and Hoodoo exploded through the doorway like men fleeing a burning building. Wearing only his shirt and drawers, Hoodoo clutched his hat, boots, breeches, and gun belt in his arms. He stubbed his toe and fell headlong just beyond the doorway, then scrambled to his feet. I saw the sentry point my way and watched as Hoodoo turned his head to follow his direction. His lips were moving, and although I couldn't hear him at that distance, I had the general notion he wasn't as happy as he might have been. The expression on his face made me glad I was as far away as I was. I watched him struggle into his clothes, face into the wind, and strike out on foot across the plain.

I was sitting near the horses with my Henry rifle in my lap when Hoodoo stumbled up onto the summit. He was gasping from the exertion, and his face was beet red. He had sweated through his shirt, and his eyes flashed like cold fire. He no longer carried his arm in a sling, and his right hand trembled near the holstered revolver at his waist. When he finally caught his breath enough to speak, he nodded toward my Henry and said, "What's the rifle for?"

"As the Mexicans say, it's 'for a precaution.' You never know—some old fool might come along and try to shoot me."

"You damn well might have it coming, by god."

Hoodoo took off his hat and mopped his brow with his sleeve. His hand was shaky as he took his canteen from the forks of his saddle, uncorked it, and drank deeply. "I suppose you think you made some kind of a point here," he said.

"Well, at least I've got you drinkin' water instead of whiskey," I replied. I was suddenly tired of the banter and the games. We had a job to do.

"Way I see it, you can make this as hard or as easy as you want it, Hawks," I said. "You can change your attitude and work with me, or you can go back to Dry Creek and draw your time."

"There's another choice," he said. "I can whip your sorry ass."

"Maybe you can, and maybe you can't. If you decide to try, you'd better bring your lunch. You'll be takin' on an all-day job."

For a long moment Hoodoo was silent. His breathing had slowed, and his face had lost some of its color. He lowered his eyes. He shrugged. When he looked at me again the anger in his face had been replaced by something like remorse. "Hell, kid," he said, "I guess I had that comin'."

It wasn't an apology, but it was close enough. "We're burning daylight," I said. "Let's ride."

We pushed west out of Fort Savage, hoping to cut the tracks of the fugitives, but we never did. I told Hoodoo of my telegraph to Marshal Ridgeway and of Major Burdette's mention of the horse ranch on Curlew Creek. Hoodoo said he knowed of George Keppler, but said no more. I didn't press him. I felt I had prodded him enough for one day.

It was just past sundown when we came to the ranch. Shadows deepened as darkness pushed back the daylight, but afterglow still lit the sky and reflected in the waters of Curlew Creek. Just beyond the shallow stream stood a low ranch house and a scatter of outbuildings.

The house was what some folks call a saddlebag house, built in the Texas style, with two log buildings separated by an open dogtrot in the middle, and the whole shebang covered by a sloping sod roof. Lamplight glowed orange in a window, and a light buckboard stood by a hitchrack out in front.

"Hello the house!" I hollered. "Anybody home?"

Inside the ranch house, a dog began to bark, high-pitched and frantic. The door opened a crack, spilling lamplight into the yard. Then a man's voice: "Who are you?"

"Merlin Fanshaw, Deputy U.S. Marshal, and Hoodoo Hawks, out of Dry Creek. All right if we come across?"

The door opened wider. The man stepped out. His left hand held a lantern high. His right hand shaded his eyes. "Come on ahead," he said.

Just then, the dog we had heard darted outside, barking sharply as it raced toward us. The animal looked to be some kind of fighting dog—a bull ter-rier, maybe. It stopped at the gravel bank of the creek, crouched low, and kept up its fierce yapping. My Rutherford horse had too much dignity to spook at a barking dog, but I could tell he wanted to. He con-tinued to step carefully, feeling his way across the rocky stream bed, but I could tell he wasn't happy about our reception committee.

"Stop that, Buster!" the man shouted. "Come here, damn you!" The dog called Buster paid him no heed at all. I was growing a little nervous myself.

Hoodoo moved up past me on his paint, riding straight toward the dog.

Hair standing stiffly along its back, the animal went into a spasm of barking that was as impressive as it was irritating. Hoodoo reined up in midstream, slowly raised his hand, and pointed his finger at the dog. He sat his horse, completely motionless, only that finger pointing.

Abruptly, the dog stopped barking. With a whimper, the animal crouched low, its head almost on the ground. Staring at Hoodoo's forefinger, the dog began to quiver. Then it scurried back to its master, tail between its legs.

Hoodoo grinned, slowly lowering the pointing finger, and we completed our crossing without further incident. It was becoming clear to me that Hoodoo Hawks was a man of diverse and mysterious abilities.

The man with the lantern scratched his head, clearly baffled. The dog cowered behind him, shivering and whimpering. "Well, I swan," he said. "I never seen old Buster behave thataway before."

Hoodoo and me reined up at the hitchrack. "I guess he just never ran into a first class dog charmer before," I said. "Would you be George Keppler?"

He nodded. "I would," he said.

Keppler squinted up at me. His face assumed an affable expression. "Deputy marshal, you say? I'm not wanted for anything, am I?"

"Not that I know of. Major Burdette, from Fort

118

Savage, said you might have horses to sell. We could maybe use a few."

Keppler's attitude changed. He ran his hand across his scalp, smoothing his thinning hair. He throwed out his chest. He smiled. "Why, yes," he said. "I do have one or two I might be willing to part with. Get down and put up your horses. You boys had supper?"

We dismounted and tied our horses to the hitchrack. "We wouldn't want to put you out none," I said.

"Not at all," Keppler said. "I was fixin' to cook up some steaks and fry some taters. How does that sound to you boys?"

Hoodoo was grinning at Buster the dog again. The animal laid its ears back and rolled over next to the cabin, showing its belly. I shook hands with Keppler. "Sounds mighty good," I told him. I caught Hoodoo's eye and by so doing probably spared the dog a heart attack. "Last feller who asked me to supper served *horse* meat, if you can believe that."

"Takes all kinds, I suppose," said Keppler. "Horses I raise are to ride. Come on inside—I'm glad to have the company."

While Keppler cooked supper, Hoodoo and me washed up in the icy waters of Curlew Creek. "What did you do to that man's dog?" I asked him.

Hoodoo grinned. "Trade secret, deputy. Us dog charmers don't like to give away our secrets."

"Little by little, I'm learning your secrets," I told

him. "I notice your bad arm seems to be workin' again."

"Just like new," he agreed, flexing his fingers. "Woman back there at the hog ranch healed me. Regular miracle worker, she was."

I grinned. "You'd best hope a cured arm is the *only* thing she gave you."

Keppler was the perfect host. He laid out a spread of beef-steak, spuds, beans and fresh bread, and Hoodoo and me showed our appreciation by packing it in with gusto. All through the meal, Keppler kept turning the conversation to horses, allowing he had the finest mounts in the territory for sale, and that he was sure he had animals that would meet our needs.

As for me, I had heard the owl and seen the elephant, and I sure hadn't just fell off the pumpkin wagon. I had been involved one way or the other in horse trades since I was twelve. I played my cards close to the vest, trying not to seem too interested. By the time supper was over, I may well have given Keppler cause to believe I was a glutton, but not a greenhorn. I praised his cooking, and thanked him for his hospitality. Then I split some kindling at the woodpile outside and filled up his wood box.

Keppler allowed we could put our horses in his small corral for the night and we did so, pulling the saddles off Rutherford and the paint and stripping the packsaddles and panniers off the packhorse. The ponies had cooled down while we were having supper, and we took them to water and then shut them in the corral and walked back to the house. Keppler said we could bunk in one of his spare rooms, but I said it being a fine evening, we would sleep out under the stars.

Before we turned in, Keppler broke out the whiskey and offered us a nightcap. I took a drink and passed the bottle back. What happened next nearly caused me to fall over from the shock. Hoodoo thanked the man, but said he had gave up drinking—on account of his religion!

Outside, I burrowed into my blankets and let my thoughts run back over the events of the day. I listened briefly to the chuckle of the creek and the patter of the cottonwood leaves. Somewhere, far off, a hoot owl called. The next thing I knowed, it was sunup.

Daybreak came soft along Curlew Creek that morning. I was awake and into my boots just as the sun topped the low hills to the east. I gave Hoodoo a nudge and said, "Daylight in the canyon, Hoodoo. Time to roll out."

"It sure don't take long to spend the night, ridin' with you," he grumbled, "but I'm up."

Woodsmoke wisped from the stovepipe over at the house, so I figured Keppler was already up and selling horses in his mind. From the hills behind the house a rider hazed a score of ponies toward the corrals. With Hoodoo, I set out to look them over.

By the time we reached the big corral, the horses

had been penned and were working out their pecking order. A moon-eyed roan bit a sorrel gelding on the neck. The sorrel squealed, kicked. Horses nearby spooked, milled, and settled down again. Corral dust, kicked up by the ponies, caught early sunlight.

I climbed to the top rail and studied the stock from that vantage point.

Most of the horses were pretty ordinary, and some were worthless skates and crow bait. But I saw one bay and a mouse-colored gray I liked. Both were short horses, deep-chested and clear-footed. I figured they'd meet our needs.

Near the corral gate, the rider who had run the horses in stood beside his cayuse, watching us. I figured he rode for Keppler, and I sized him up with some care, all the while pretending to study the livestock. The man was small and wiry, brown as a tobacco plug, with bright, hard eyes and a thin moustache. A ragged scar ran down his cheek, from just in front of his ear to his jawline. He wore shotgun shaps, big-roweled Spanish spurs, and a belted six-shooter. I know we're not supposed to judge by appearances, but the gent had all the earmarks of a bona fide hardcase.

I stepped down off the corral. "Good mornin'," I said. The man made no answer, but nodded.

I offered him my hand. "I'm Merlin Fanshaw, out of Dry Creek. Do you ride for Keppler?" Again, he made no reply. He didn't take my hand. He smiled, but his eyes didn't.

122

"I asked you—do you ride for Keppler?"

He shrugged. *"No habla ingles."*

"Oh." I said. What I thought was, "I'll bet you can *habla* just about all the *ingles* you choose to."

Right then George Keppler ambled up, bright and friendly as the sunrise. "Good mornin', boys," he said. "I see you met Rafael. Appears you couldn't wait to look my horses over."

"We are in sort of a hurry," I said.

"Well, then. Them animals is the cream of the crop. You see anything there you like?"

"Maybe," I said. "I don't have time to horse-trade with you, so I'll just lay my cards on the table. I like that bay gelding and the gray. How much?"

Keppler stretched his neck and looked into the corral like he'd never seen the horses before. He stroked his jaw and assumed a pensive look. "You've got a good eye for horseflesh, Deputy. Them two are about the best I've got. I ain't sure I can part with 'em."

"Like I said, I'm in a hurry. How much?"

"Well. It would be a sacrifice, but I could maybe let 'em go for, say—two hundred a head."

"I expect you could," I said, "seein' as they're only worth maybe seventy-five each. Throw in a couple of halters and I'll give you a hundred dollars a head."

Keppler gave me a hard look. "Tell you what, Deputy. You need horses, and I've got 'em to sell. I'm the only man inside of fifteen miles who does. Way I see it, you're over a barrel. My price just went up to two hundred and fifty each."

I grinned. "Your price is goin' up when it should be comin' down, Keppler. I could requisition them ponies, you know. Federal law gives me the right."

The man called Rafael stepped out into the sunlight. His hand hung close to that holstered revolver I'd noticed. Keppler nodded. "Yes, I suppose you could," he said, "but are you sure you're ready for that, Deputy?"

From behind me, I heard Hoodoo's voice. "I don't believe we want any of these nags, Merlin."

My eyes still on Keppler and Rafael, I asked, "Oh? Why not?"

"Well," Hoodoo drawled, "the truth is, I recognize some of the brands them animals are wearin.' They belong to local ranchers hereabouts. Ain't but three or four wearin' your mark, Keppler."

Keppler's eyes widened, then narrowed to slits. Hoodoo had struck a nerve. "That is interesting," I said. "I expect you have bills of sale for all those horses."

I saw doubt flicker across Keppler's face. I turned, let the sunlight reflect off my badge. For a moment I thought the man would try to push it, but in the end he lost his nerve.

"I—I ain't sure I've got papers for all of 'em," he said. "Besides, like you say, you're in a hurry. Tell you what, Deputy. I aim to be a good citizen— you can have the bay and the gray for a hundred each, cash."

And so the deal was made. I pulled out my roll, peeled a couple of hundred dollar greenbacks off the top, and handed the money to Keppler. I noticed Rafael's eyes widen as he took note of my tinhorn bankroll, and it did give me pleasure. He might not *habla ingles,* I thought, but he seems to *habla* cash money, all right. I sensed Hoodoo's disapproval of my grandstanding, but I ignored him. Of course, I could have given Keppler a note from Uncle Sam, but I was showing off, playing the high roller.

Keppler carefully folded the bank notes and stuck them in his pocket. He squinted up at me. "A pleasure doing business with you," he said. "What brings you boys out this way, if you don't mind my askin'?"

"Looking for two men and a woman. Riding thoroughbred horses. Didn't see such come through here today, did you?"

He shook his head. "No," he said. "Hasn't been anyone through here all week."

Keppler gave me bills of sale for the horses, and Hoodoo and me hit the trail with two fresh mounts. Long shadows stretched out before us as we headed west toward the Pryor Mountains. "I'm glad you noticed those ponies were wearin' local brands," I told Hoodoo. "You sure called Keppler's bluff."

"There's bluffs and there's bluffs," Hoodoo said. "Truth is, I never recognized *any* of them brands."

nine

We hadn't rode more than a mile when we noticed a rider coming up fast behind us. Hoodoo looked through his spyglass and spat. "It's Keppler's man," he said, "Rafael."

"Wonder what he wants."

Hoodoo closed up the spyglass and returned it to his saddlebag. "Probably Keppler decided you overpaid him for the horses, and he's sending his hired hand with a refund."

"Yeah," I said. "That'll be the day."

We reined up and waited. I wasn't expecting any trouble, but I did make sure I could lay hands on my .44 if I should need it in a hurry. The rider slowed his horse to a walk, raising his hand in greeting. He smiled.

I wasn't much good at speaking Spanish, but I gave it a try. "*Hola,* Rafael," I said. "*Que paso?*"

The little man rode closer and drew rein. He smiled again, but he didn't meet my eyes. There were fresh spur marks on the flanks of his lathered horse and old scars as well. I decided I didn't like Rafael all that much.

"*Hola!*" he said. Still smiling, he looked first at Hoodoo and then back at me. I expect his smile was meant to be affable, but it just made him look like a skulker.

He licked his lips. "You know them peoples you ask about? I seen them maybe."

"You don't say. You speak pretty good English for a man who don't *habla.*" I was getting tired of his smile.

"I think I should tell you maybe," he said, "about the men. And the woman."

"I'm listening."

Rafael bowed his head, his eyes sly beneath the shadow of his hat. "Maybe there is a small reward," he said. The thumb and fingers of his hand rubbed together in the age-old sign.

"You tell me what you know," I said, "and I'll tell you what it's worth."

His face fell. He was silent for a moment. Then he shrugged. "They came through about noon yesterday. *Dos hombres*—two men—and a woman. *Muy guapo.* Very pretty."

"What kind of horses were they riding?"

"*Los hombres*—the men—rode a bay and a chestnut. *La señorita* rode a black."

I looked at Hoodoo. He caught my glance, then dropped his eyes. Rafael was smiling his oily smile again. "Sounds like the folks we're lookin' for, all right," I said. "Which way did they go?"

"They circle around north of the ranch, then go south."

"I appreciate your coming forward," I said. "I'd say that information is worth—oh, ten dollars, say."

His face fell. His mouth took on a sullen look. "I think maybe *more.*"

"*I* think you'd do well to take the ten dollars. We just might go back to Keppler's with you and look at those horse brands again."

Rafael took the ten. He turned his horse around, back the way he'd come. "*Gracias,*" he said, "*por nada.*" Then he spurred the little cayuse hard and rode away at a high lope.

Hoodoo looked thoughtful. "I spent some time in this country a few years back," he said. "Traded with the Crow. No ranches then. No white men at all, except a few trappers and traders. Thing I recall is how scarce water is along through here."

"There's been creeks," I said. "Sidewinder Creek at the fort. Curlew Creek back at Keppler's."

"Yes. There's others, too. Some muddy, some alkali, some dry. What I mean to say is there's not that much *good* water. Not until you get to the mountains, anyway. Rafael said the riders and the girl came through yesterday about noon. They circled around Keppler's ranch and headed south, according to him."

"We could go back north of Keppler's and try to pick up their trail."

"That would mean turnin' back. Losin' time. What I'm sayin' is I know where most of the good springs are. The Bozeman Trail ain't but twelve miles or so from here. There's a spring right off the trail that has a steady flow of clean, sweet water year around. Immigrant wagons used to stop, fill their barrels there.

"If the men we're after are familiar with the country

128

at all, they'll head for that spring. They don't know we're on their trail, so they might even figure to camp there a day or two."

"And if they're not there?"

"Then we've missed them. Could be they're headed for those mountains yonder. Them on the right is the Pryors—that high point would be Crown Butte. To the left is the Big Horn range. Beyond lies Wyoming."

"You're the tracker," I told him. "Lead on."

It was maybe one o'clock when we stopped for a cold lunch in a brushy coulee just off the trail. The day had grown hotter as the sun climbed to its midday point, and the mountains to the south seemed to shimmer in the heat waves. The air was still, and the day had taken on a sultry mood that made a man feel drowsy and dull. It would have been easy to grow careless under such conditions, but I knew we dare not let down our guard.

Someplace up ahead were two desperate men and Julie. Even a moment's carelessness could lead to consequences I'd rather not have to pay.

Above the mountains, thunderclouds gathered, building on themselves to rise high and flat-topped in a sky so blue it hurt the eyes. Storms could blow up fast in that country, bringing lightning, rain, and maybe hail. Flash floods could follow, turning a dry coulee into a muddy torrent that carried sagebrush, rock, prairie dogs, and such before it with the speed of an express train. Then the storm would end, and the land would once again bake under the summer sun.

Hoodoo didn't talk at all during the time it took to wolf down the cold biscuits and jerked beef we'd taken from the pannier. He had already talked more that day than any time since I'd knowed him. He hunkered in the sunshine well apart from where I sat, just thinking. I did the same.

I have never been particularly gifted with second sight, or if I have I guess I don't know how to recognize it. Like most everyone else, there have been times in my life when I felt fearful for no reason I could put a name to. Sometimes I've had a powerful feeling that someone I was close to was in terrible danger, but I was powerless to help because I didn't know what the danger was or what help was needed.

Sometimes I simply had a hunch that kept me from taking a particular trail or caused me to avoid some person. I don't know if it was watching the storm clouds build that day or if it was because Julie was strong on my mind, but the feeling came over me that some terrible calamity lay ahead.

I stood up suddenly, trying to shake the feeling. Catching my movement, Hoodoo turned and looked my way. "Let's get horseback," I said. "Storm's a-comin'."

We moved steadily south. Overhead, stormclouds gathered and the sky grew dark. In the distance, bright lightning stabbed, startling the eyes. Thunder rolled with a sound like gravel shoveled onto a drum. A cold wind swept in. My Rutherford horse didn't like the coming storm any better than I did. He tossed his head and did a nervous little quickstep as if to say he wouldn't be all that unhappy if I found him a nice, cozy barn somewhere.

I drew rein and stepped down. My yellow slicker was rolled and tied behind the cantle of my saddle. I untied the saddle strings and pulled the garment on while the wind rattled the oiled canvas and whipped the tails around my legs. Ahead, Hoodoo turned in the saddle to watch me, then stepped down off his paint and followed suit.

The rain began to pelt down, huge drops the size of sparrow eggs that splattered when they struck. I made my way to Hoodoo and put a hand on his shoulder. I had to shout to make him hear me. "Should we look for shelter and hole up?"

He shook his head. "No. We need to move on. The spring is only about three miles from here. If the kidnappers are there, they'll be hunkered down against the storm. Maybe too busy to notice us."

I nodded. As I've said, I wasn't much of a praying man in those days, but I said a prayer that day. It went something like: "Lord—please don't let me get into anything this day that you and me together can't get me out of." Now I know that don't sound all that religious, but it came from the heart.

For most of the next mile or so I felt like a turtle beneath a waterfall. The rain grew heavier as the

131

prairie turned to mud, and then the powers up yonder in charge of rainfall dumped the whole load. I could see no farther than Rutherford's ears; the rest of the world was water. Rain rattled and spattered off my slicker and hat, Rutherford struggled to keep his footing on the rainslick earth, and I couldn't see Hoodoo or our other horses at all.

Then, almost as soon as the storm had begun, it stopped. The dark clouds broke, and the sun came out on a fresh-washed prairie that sparkled like a field of diamonds. Hoodoo and the horses came into view again. The clean, pungent smell of sage struck my nostrils. Everything seemed bright and new-minted, as if the world had been reborn. And still the heavy feeling that had earlier come upon me remained. Was this sense of dread some kind of warning? Or was it all just my nerves?

I dismounted and took off my slicker, tying it again behind the cantle of my saddle. Ahead, Hoodoo drew rein and stepped down, waiting for me to come up. Leading Rutherford, I walked through the wet grass to where he stood. As I approached, he placed a finger to his lips as a signal for silence. When he spoke, it was in a whisper.

"The spring is just ahead, beyond that low hill. We can hobble the horses and leave them here. We just might take them fellers by surprise."

I nodded. "How does the land lay?"

"Long, grassy bench, open to the south. The spring has formed a washed out area six or eight feet lower than the high ground. If the gents we're huntin' are camped there, they'll be above on the bench."

I pulled my old Henry rifle from its scabbard and levered a shell into its chamber. "All right," I said. "Let's go."

I saw the horses first. Crouched low, we had made our stalk around the hill. Now, screened from view by a patch of scrub cedar, we began a careful approach from the north. Just ahead the bank dropped off sharply, and I could hear the splashing sound of the spring. Above, on the grassy bench, grazed the chestnut and the bay. Julie's black stood, somewhat apart from the others, also feeding on the good, tall grass. All three horses were saddled, but only Julie's black wore hobbles.

The animals had been used hard, and they showed it. They looked thin, their coats tousled and rough. Their owners had removed their bridles so the animals could graze more freely. Intent on their feeding, the horses seemed unaware of our presence.

Beside me, Hoodoo peered through the branches of the cedar, his Sharps buffalo gun in his hands, as motionless as any statue. I lay on my belly, holding my Henry with sweaty palms. My breathing was rapid and shallow. The beating of my heart was so loud in my ears I thought for a moment it might give us away.

Hoodoo drew out the spyglass from the buckskin coat that he wore. He opened it and began a slow scan of the bench. I held my breath, waiting. Then I heard, faintly at first, a sound I scarcely could credit. It was the sound of someone ahead, at the spring below us— a woman's voice—and she was *singing!*

I held my breath, the better to hear her. Could the voice be Julie's? Now I could make out the words. They belonged to an old song, a fast-paced ballad I had ofttimes heard in bunkhouse and barroom—"The Gypsy Davy."

Bright and sweet as a meadowlark's warble, the sound drifted up to us as we lay in the grass behind the cedar:

> *"Well, have you forsaken your house and home?*
> *Have you forsaken your baby?*
> *Have you forsaken your husband dear*
> *To go with the Gypsy Davy,*
> *And sing with the Gypsy Dave?"*

From the look on Hoodoo's face, he couldn't believe his ears. The last thing a person would expect to hear in such a wild and remote place would be a young woman singing! We still could not see the singer, but we heard the song plainly.

> *"Yes, I've forsaken my house and home*
> *To go with the Gypsy Davy,*
> *And I'll forsake my husband dear*
> *But not my blue-eyed baby,*
> *Not my blue-eyed babe."*

I eased over past Hoodoo and slid down through the grass behind the cedars, hoping to get a view of the songstress at the spring. That's when the bottom dropped out, and the whole world turned upside down!

Several things happened at nearly the same time. I tried to stop my slide but could not on the still-wet grass; I lost hold of my Henry repeater and pitched headlong over the bank!

Julie McAllister knelt at a pool below where the waters cascaded from the rocks. She wore only her shift and was in the act of bathing her arms and face with a cloth. Her eyes went wide as she saw me falling toward her from above. On the bench across from us, Julie's black horse raised its head and whinnied! Two men, dressed in black, stepped out of the cedars. The taller of the two pointed toward Julie and me, pulling his gun at the same time! And Hoodoo Hawks fired his Sharps at the men with a sound like the crack of doom!

Now if you're wondering how I could take in all these events while falling off a bank, let me come right out and admit that I could not. It was only later, looking back on the action of that split-second of time and with Hoodoo's help, that I was able to put them together.

Julie's hat and clothes had been laid beside her on a rock. She snatched them up, clutching them to her bosom, as she stared at me. I think she screamed, but I can't be sure of that. I landed half in and half out of the pool at the base of the spring with a thump that knocked the wind out of me but did no other harm. The two men on the slope above had pulled their pistols and were firing both at me and at Hoodoo above me. I had lost my rifle and would have drawed my .44 except that I couldn't breathe. In the end I just laid where I'd fallen, gasping like a trout on a riverbank.

Hoodoo must still have been where we had lain behind the cedar. I heard him fire again, the gunfire just above Julie and me and sounding loud as cannon fire. Julie dropped to the ground beside me and stared at my face as if she couldn't believe her eyes. She looked plumb astonished as she asked, "Merlin?" I was glad she recognized me. I surely would have replied if I was able.

The firing became general. At last, I got my wind back. I sucked in air, throwed my arm across Julie's back, and held her close beside me as bullets spung into the bank and tore the air above us. Then, suddenly, the shooting stopped. I heard Hoodoo's voice, calling my name. "Fanshaw!" he shouted. "You all right?"

I shouted back. "Yeah! I'm fine!"

Then Hoodoo's voice again, weaker this time. "Well, get your arse up here then. I've been hit."

The first thing I noticed when I got to my feet was that the men on the bench and their horses were nowhere to be seen. Julie's black was still there, but the kidnappers had vanished. As for Julie herself, she stared wide-eyed at me from where she knelt by the spring. Her bath had been wasted; when I pulled her down beside me I had pretty well wallered her around in the mud.

Hoodoo's voice from above the springs reminded me of my priorities. "No hurry, Deputy," he said. "If you wait down there long enough I'll be beyond your help."

I scrambled up the bank to find him sitting in the grass, trying to stanch a bleeding wound in his thigh. "The short bastard shot me when I stood up," he said. "but I harbor no hard feelin's. I was tryin' hard to shoot *him* at the time."

"My fault," I said. "If I hadn't fell off the dern bank—"

"—you probably would have just got in my way," he finished.

I lifted his hand to look at the wound. There was an ugly hole and an abundance of blood, but the slug had missed both the artery and the bone. The bullet had passed through and had put him down, but he would recover. What I didn't tell him was that I had suffered a similar wound myself back in '82. The reason I didn't tell him was that I had shot myself by accident on that occasion, but that's another story. I'm not going to tell *you* about it either.

Hoodoo's eyes stared past me. I turned and there was Julie. Hoodoo looked embarrassed, and his glib and wicked tongue was nowhere to be found. He tried to sit up straighter, and his hands covered the wound again.

"Now, miss," he said, "you don't want to see this."

Julie had donned her riding skirt, blouse, and boots. She took one look at Hoodoo, removed her blouse, and knelt beside him. "Don't be silly," she said. "I've doctored my dad and any number of cowboys in my time. Sometimes I think the thing you men do best is get yourselves hurt."

Hoodoo's face had turned crimson. Julie lifted his hands away, as I had done, and appraised the damage. "Not that bad," she told him. "The bleeding has slowed down. You're probably feeling a little light-headed right now."

Julie turned to me. "We can use my blouse as a bandage," she said, "but first we need to clean the wound properly. Do you have any whiskey?"

I looked at Hoodoo and grinned. "I don't know, but I'll bet we do."

If it had been just him and me I reckon he would have told me to go to hell, but he wouldn't let himself cuss in front of Julie. I could barely hear him when he answered. "In my saddlebags."

Together, Julie and I probed the wound and rinsed it with whiskey. Hoodoo grunted and the cords in his neck stood out like cables. "First time whiskey ever hurt me without makin' me feel good first," he said.

"This time it's the other way around," Julie said. "This time it hurts first and will help you feel good after."

She held the bottle up to the light. It was still nearly a third full. Julie favored Hoodoo with her brightest smile. "The patient can have the rest," she said, "but the doctor comes first." She tipped the bottle up, drank deeply, and passed it on to me. Then, looking into my eyes, she said, "Thanks for the rescue, Merlin."

ten

I walked over to the long slope where we had first seen Julie's kidnappers and looked out across the valley. There was no sign of the men or their horses. Hoodoo's rifle fire must have made them think we were a bigger party than we were. The outlaws had broke off the fight and quit the country. They had left Julie behind, but they had ridden away with $10,000 of her daddy's money in their saddle-bags. Some days it's hard to keep believing that crime don't pay.

I took the hobbles off Julie's mare and led the animal back to where Hoodoo lay behind the cedars. Julie knelt at his side. She looked up as I drew rein. "He's still hurting," she said, "but the whiskey should help."

From what I knowed of Hoodoo that was like saying water would help a frog. "Oh, yes," I said, "I expect it will."

With Julie's aid, I got the packhorse unloaded and

the other ponies staked out to graze. In a cotton-wood grove just west of the springs I found sufficient deadwood for a fire, and before long we had coffee brewing and beans and bacon cooking in the Dutch oven. Julie sat across the fire from me, looking at herself in a small mirror she'd taken from her saddlebag, and tried to comb the tangles from her long, dark hair.

I had given her a spare shirt from my warbag to replace the blouse she'd used to bandage Hoodoo. The garment never looked better, nor ever would, than it did that day on her.

She looked into my eyes and smiled. "I'm so glad you're all right," she said. "When that man—that Vince Coldwater—hit you with his rifle butt back at Alkali Springs, I was afraid you might have been badly hurt. It was brave of you to stand up to them on my account."

"Oh, not really," I said. "I just got mad, I reckon. I was afraid for you."

The coffee had come to a rolling boil. Julie took the pot from the fire and poured in a cup of cold water to settle the grounds. "I was afraid myself at first," she said, "but the men never harmed or mistreated me. They told me when Daddy paid the ransom money they'd set me free."

"That's what got me so riled," I said. "I brought the money, but they wouldn't turn you loose."

Julie poured a cup of coffee and handed it to me. "And by the way," I said, "those fellers may have claimed to be Vince and Cletus Coldwater, but according to Hoodoo, they're not."

"They're not? Then why would they pretend they were?"

I sipped my coffee and thought about her question. "Maybe they wanted to throw the blame on the Coldwaters. Vince and Clete are well-known desperados in the territory, and they have been seen lately in our neck of the woods."

Julie reached for the coffee pot and poured a cup for herself. There was mud on her riding skirt and her boots, and there was a smudge of ashes from the fire on her cheek. Even so, to my mind she was pretty as a May morning. I asked the question I'd been wondering about. "How did they come to take you, Julie?"

She frowned, remembering. "I'd gone riding in the hills above the ranch. I did that almost every day. I used to ride across those open parks and through the timber. Sometimes I'd take a book along and do some reading.

"I don't know how those men knew I was there. Maybe they'd been watching me. Anyway, on that particular day, suddenly, there they were. They said they were taking me so Daddy would buy my freedom. Daddy and I hadn't been on good terms for some time—I remember thinking he might not pay them."

"You've got your dad all wrong," I said. "The last thing he said to me before we left Dry Creek was 'I don't care a damn about the money, but don't you let anything happen to my little girl!'"

Julie's hand trembled slightly as she brought her cup to her lips. There were tears in her eyes, and it wasn't from the campfire smoke. "I do love him," she said. "Daddy's an old bear, but I know he cares for me. Maybe it's just that we're too much alike. We're both proud, stubborn, and willful."

I put another length of wood on the fire and lifted the lid of the Dutch oven. The beans and bacon were simmering away in fine style. I felt Julie's eyes on me. "How did you get involved in all this?" she asked.

"When the ransom note came, your dad sent for Chance Ridgeway, the U.S. Marshal from over at Silver City. I guess they've been friends for a long time. Ridgeway said he's your godfather."

Julie nodded. "Yes. He also stood up for my mother and dad when they got married. I've known Dad Ridgeway all my life."

"Well, I haven't knowed him that long. I met him back in '82, the year my pa died. Ridgeway asked for my help in a case he was working on, and sort of took me under his wing. When you were kidnapped he offered me a job as deputy."

She glanced over at the sleeping form of Hoodoo Hawks. "And him?" she asked.

I grinned. "Hoodoo Hawks. Indian scout, range detective, and tracker. The marshal figured I needed someone to help me find you. We didn't get along all that well at first, but we're beginning to grow on each other."

She smiled; then the smile faded. "And now he's been shot—because of me."

Above the collar of my old shirt, Julie's skin was smooth as ivory. "Not because of you," I said. "Because of greedy men. Because of outlaws."

Julie looked at the beans and bacon again and moved them from the coals. "You're sweet, Merlin," she said. "How about some dinner?"

"You bet," I said. "Eating is one of the things I do best."

Julie took Hoodoo a plate of bacon and beans, a cup of coffee, and some fry bread she'd cooked in a skillet. Strain showed on the old tracker's face, and it was clear his leg was causing him considerable discomfort. "How are you feeling, Mr. Hawks?" asked Julie.

"*Mr.* Hawks!" Hoodoo said, "I ain't been 'mistered' since I got drunk at the Methodist picnic! Call me 'Hoodoo,' girl."

Julie chuckled. " 'Hoodoo' it is," she said. "You can call *me* 'doctor.' "

Hoodoo laughed out loud, a joyful guffaw that startled me. Since we'd been on the trail together I'd scarcely seen the man smile. "That's right," he said. "You gave me the shirt off your back and played patty-finger in my blood. You poured good whiskey on my leg, and passed the bottle around. You're my kind of doctor, girl!"

143

Hoodoo sat up atop the bedroll, his wounded leg straight out. He took the plate Julie offered. "First hot food I've et since we left Dry Creek," he said. "The deputy yonder wouldn't let us stop long enough to cook a decent meal. Kept pushin' to catch up with them hardcases and find you." He breathed in the aroma of the food and looked up at Julie. "Now," he said, "I understand why." Smiling, Julie turned and looked at me as if she'd never seen me before. I grinned and commenced to eat.

Daylight seems to last forever in the summertime. The days don't pass so much as they mellow, and the light walks stately from sunup through the glare of midday to the soft shadows of twilight. With the approach of nightfall the sky above our small camp turned gold, then rose, and blazed red before fading to gray.

I took the horses to water, then set them out for the night, tethered by stake rope or cumbered by hobbles. I let the packhorse graze free, for he was an old and steady animal, not inclined to adventure. He would stay with the others, for horses love the company of their own kind even more than people do.

The evening came in on a cool breeze from the mountains, and I knew the night would be pleasant after the heat of the day. I divided the blankets and quilts from the bedroll three ways, giving Julie and Hoodoo the best of it. I wondered where Julie had slept since she'd been taken by the kidnappers, and I asked her. She said at first she'd been kept at a cabin west of Dry Creek, and that since Alkali Springs she had slept under her saddle blanket. She said she was glad the weather had been good, and thanked me for the bedding.

Julie slept nearest the fire. Hoodoo lay in the soogans, under the tarp. I made my bed atop the pack-saddle pads with my saddle for a pillow, not far from Hoodoo. I was pretty sure we were in no danger from the kidnappers—they had their ransom money, after all—but I staked Rutherford close by anyway, and kept my Henry within easy reach just to be on the safe side.

The stars came out, just one or two, here and there. Then, as the sky darkened, they appeared by the thousands. I laid back, listening to the sounds of the night—the muffled thud of the horses' hooves as they grazed, the sound of their chewing, the snap of the dying embers of our fire. From somewhere far in the distance came the high-pitched babble of a coyote choir. Overhead, in the deepening darkness, a nightbird cried.

I took the hobbles off my thoughts and let them drift. Hoodoo and me had done what we set out to do—we had delivered the ransom, and we had recovered Julie. We'd had a brief skirmish with the kidnappers, but no one had been hurt, except for Hoodoo. I felt bad about him getting shot, but he was a tough old bird. I had every reason to believe he would heal quickly.

Julie was just as I remembered her, and more. She was her father's daughter, in spite of their differences, strong, brave, and proud. In my mind I had pictured her as the opposite of those qualities. I had imagined her frightened, wringing her hands and weeping. I had thought her weak and needy. Julie was neither of those things.

It was only an impression, I guess, but sometimes, especially when she spoke of her dad, it almost seemed Julie didn't want to go home.

I remembered the day I overheard their argument at the ranch. I recalled Thane's angry, ugly words, and the defiance in Julie's voice. I knew those two had got themselves into a place of conflict, and that neither of them knew how to back away. It made me sad, just thinking about it.

I was glad everything had worked out so well, but now I was glad for a more personal reason. Until I took Julie back to the ranch I would be spending time in her company. Somehow that thought made all the worry and the risk worthwhile.

I decided we would camp there at the springs for a few days, in order to allow Hoodoo time to heal up some and to give the horses a rest. I would be able to talk with Julie, share my thoughts with her, as we never could have done back at Dry Creek.

I looked up at the night sky and saw a shooting star streak across the blackness, like God striking a sulfur match. Then I pulled the blanket up around my ears and drifted off to sleep.

After we'd had breakfast the next morning, I asked Julie if she'd care to take a ride with me and look over the country some. She allowed that she would, after she'd cleaned up a mite. I watched her walk away down to the springs with towel, comb, and that small mirror she used. She walked through the still-wet grass and sagebrush with confidence and style and dropped out of sight below the bank.

Hoodoo looked worn and tired when I went to check on his wound. He lay back on the bed tarp and offered his thigh for me to examine. "Hurts like hell this mornin'," he said. "I suppose you'll tell me that's a good sign."

"It's a sign you took a bullet in your leg," I said. "Healing takes time."

"Go away," he grumbled. "Send that doctor girl over. She makes me laugh."

"I expect she'll stop by when she gets back from the springs. Then her and me are going for a ride. We aim to explore the country some."

"A ride? You mean just roamin' around for no reason?"

"*Got* a reason. I might do some hunting—maybe get us some fresh meat."

Hoodoo's expression turned skeptical. "Huntin', huh? Seems to me you've already *found* what *you're* huntin'."

When Julie came walking toward me that morning, leading her black mare, she looked much as she had that day at the ranch when she'd watched me ride the sorrel. Her pearl gray Stetson shaded her eyes, and her hair fell from beneath its brim like a waterfall. She wore her black wool vest over the shirt I had given her. Tight-fitting gloves of deerskin adorned her hands. She had brushed the mud from her riding skirt, and silver-mounted spurs set off her custom-made boots. Julie smiled her bright smile as she approached, and I believe at that moment there's nothing she could have asked of me that I wouldn't have tried to accomplish.

I would have worked as a clerk at a dry goods store, wearing a boiled shirt and a derby hat. I would have held up a lightning rod on a mountain peak during a thunderstorm. I would have stood between a sow grizzly and her cubs. In short, I would have done just about anything the girl wanted, just to see her smile.

What I said was, "You don't look half bad, once you tidy up some." That made her smile again, which only encouraged me. I said, "Fact is, you look a lot different than you did when I dropped off the bank in the middle of your bath. You were singing 'The Gypsy Davy,' as I recall."

She laughed. "You were the *last* thing I expected to see right then! I had asked the Coldwaters—or who-ever they are—if I could wash up a bit, and the man who called himself 'Vince' said 'Go ahead. The horses need rest anyway.' Then he and the other man stretched out on the grassy slope to rest. As for the song, I was singing to keep my spirits up."

She had saddled her black mare. Preparing to mount, she gripped the reins atop the animal's neck. I said, "Your horse looks more rested today, too."

"Yes," Julie said, "I thought I'd ride her this morning. We won't be out long, will we?"

"Maybe an hour or two. A little exercise will keep her from getting stiff."

Julie swung up into the saddle with one easy movement. "Then let's go. We can talk as we ride."

I stepped up onto Rutherford, and rode out with Julie by my side.

We followed a game trail southwest from our camp, drifting along through greasewood and scrub cedar to a steep slope that overlooked the valley. The land rolled away in a series of low hills toward the limestone cliffs and spires of the Pryor Mountains. Fleecy clouds passed overhead like clipper ships at sea, and their shadows flowed beneath, sliding up and down the hills and rippling over the land.

Julie and me rode side by side when the trail would allow, single file when it would not. We turned up a long hill topped by windswept pines, and spooked a big mule deer from his bed. The buck exploded out and down the slope in that stiff-legged bounce peculiar to the breed and left Rutherford and Julie's mare quivering with surprise. My Henry rifle was in its saddle scabbard, but I made no move to reach for it. My "hunting" story was just an excuse for the ride, and Hoodoo knew it.

The hill grew steeper, dropping off into a shadowed canyon. Just off the crest, the slope fell sharply to a narrow ledge thirty feet below. Spires of limestone thrust up out of the incline, bounded by sliderock and scree as far down as the ledge. Beyond the rim was a sheer drop of two hundred feet or more to the canyon floor.

By the time Julie and me reached the top of the hill, the horses were nearly winded. We reined up and dismounted to let them catch their breath.

Looking out at the fast-moving clouds and their shadows on the land, I said, "When I was a kid, and saw those clouds sail past like that, I used to pretend I was standing on the bottom of the ocean, looking up at the ships on its surface. I knew nothing about the ocean, you understand; I had never even seen a good-sized lake. But I enjoyed thinking about oceans. I liked to imagine how it would be to be a mermaid—or a mer-man—who lived at the bottom of the sea.

"Later, I came to love books about the sea, especially books about ships and pirates and such. I once gave an outlaw chief Mr. Dana's book, *Two Years Before The Mast*. The outlaw was an old rip, but he loved to read. He's in territorial prison now, but I expect he's still a reader.

"Anyway, I love books—all kinds. What brought all that to mind was when you talked about carrying books with you to read on your rides above the ranch. I wondered whether you had a book with you the day them fellers kidnapped you, and if that book was a comfort to you."

Julie smiled. "I was just going to *ask* if you liked books! I knew you did! Yes! I did have a book that day, and yes, it did help. I like poetry. Poets—good poets—give form to things we can't describe for ourselves.

"I have that book with me now—it's called *Sonnets from the Portuguese*, by Elizabeth Barrett Browning. It's my favorite!"

Julie seemed excited as a schoolgirl as she crossed swiftly to the mare and reached into her saddlebag. She took out a small, leather-bound volume and turned back to me, the book open. She handed it to me, pointing to the open page. "This one is about a woman's love," she said. "It begins: 'How do I love thee? Let me count the ways—"

I don't know how it happened. I reached to take the slim volume Julie was handing me, and somehow our hands collided. The book flew out into space, over the edge of the hill, its pages fluttering like the wings of a falling dove, and landed thirty feet below on the ledge. For a moment, we both stood looking down at where the book had come to rest. It lay in the scree and loose rock, perilously close to the edge.

Julie's face looked stricken. "I-I'm sorry, Julie," I said, "I must have knocked it out of your hand. I'm really sorry—"

But I knew that sorry wasn't good enough. The book was her favorite, she'd said. Its verses had cheered and

151

consoled her both before her kidnapping and after. I had to get it back for her. My catchrope lay coiled at the forks of my saddle, and I reached for it. The lariat was a forty-foot length of hard-twist Manila rope, and I was never without it. I could use it to lower myself down to the ledge and retrieve the book.

The stump of an ancient pine stood beside the trail, gnarled roots clinging to the ridge. I tightened the loop over the stump, tied the other end around my waist, and stepped to the edge. "Don't worry," I told Julie, "I'll just go down and fetch it back."

"Oh, Merlin," she said, "Are you sure? That slope looks awfully steep."

It *was* awfully steep. I can't say I didn't have a few misgivings about stepping off into space that way, but I could do no less. With my feet braced against the incline, I leaned back, hoping the lariat would hold me. Looking back on it now, I can't imagine why I thought it might not. That rope had held everything from longhorn steers to fighting mustangs without breaking. I suppose I was a mite uneasy because what I was asking of it on that occasion was a good deal more *personal*.

My feet walked me backward down the slope as I leaned against the taut line and tried to concentrate on the task at hand. Loose rock and dirt, dislodged by my boots, crumbled and clattered away beneath me, bouncing down off the ledge and out into space. The hammering of my heart was loud in my ears, and for a time there I forgot to breathe.

I had nearly reached the end of my rope, as the saying goes, when I felt the earth level off beneath me. My feet stood on the surface of the ledge. Carefully, I turned, reaching for Julie's volume of poems. The rope was tight as a fiddle string. Stretching against its pull, I touched the book, and with some scratching and straining managed to pick it up.

My hands were trembling. I looked up to see if Julie was watching from the trail above, but she was not. Only the white clouds against the deep blue of the sky showed atop the ridge. I jammed the book down the front of my britches, took a deep breath, and made ready to climb back to the top. That's when my plans took a turn for the worse. Suddenly, the lariat dropped from above in a loose tangle—loop, honda, and all!

I thought I heard Julie call my name. She cried, "Merlin!" her voice sounding frightened. I called out in answer, "Julie! Are you all right?" I called again, and a third time, but no answer came at all.

eleven

What had happened? I stood perplexed on the narrow shelf, leaning into the hillside. The coils of my lariat lay at my feet where they'd fallen. The rope had not broken. Something—*someone*—had removed it from the stump above and let it fall. But who? Had the kidnappers come back? Or had some new threat taken Julie by surprise?

Surely, she would have seen a man coming up the trail. Could someone have been hiding atop the hill? I had questions aplenty, but dern few answers.

I moved, hugging the incline. Sliderock and scree cascaded over the rim of the ledge and into the canyon below me. Maybe, I thought, I can climb back to the top. Carefully, I dug the toe of my boot into the slope, seeking a foothold. I dug my fingers into the hillside. Gingerly, I put my weight on my foot. Loose rock moved beneath me; I felt myself slipping backward toward the edge!

My slide stopped, just short of the rim. Sweat stung my eyes. The rapid pulsing of my heart was loud in my ears. I held my breath, afraid to move. "Think, Merlin, think!" I told myself, "There has to be a way out of this!"

I glanced down at the ledge beneath my feet. It extended along the hillside, wider in some places than others. "Well," I thought, "If I can't climb up from here, maybe I can ease sideways along the bench, and find a way to the top." Carefully, I moved left along the ledge, clinging to the rocky slope like a crab. My progress was ever so slow, but at length I came to a place broad enough to stand on while I caught my breath. Slowly, I wiped the sweat from my eyes with my shirtsleeve, and coiled my lariat.

A hawk glided past, riding the currents above the canyon. The bird seemed to look at me in its flight as if to say, "What the hell are you doing up here in my domain?" I would have been glad to leave it, I thought, if only I knowed how.

I surely couldn't use my lariat to lower myself down. Forty feet of rope would still leave me a hundred and sixty feet or so short of the bottom. Well, I thought, maybe I can throw a loop on something above me, something solid enough to hold my weight and allow me to clamber up. "Yes," my skeptical side answered, "and maybe you can't."

Forty feet farther along, the outcropping that formed the ledge extended sharply out over the canyon, then curved back in. When I reached that point, I looked up and saw a nubbin of limestone, maybe a foot thick, jutting out from the hilltop. I had always considered myself a fair hand with a catch rope, but I knew the rock would be a difficult throw at best. I had a few other questions, too. If I did manage to rope it, would the rock hold my weight? The catch would require me to throw a loop almost straight up. Could I do so without losing my balance and falling off the ledge? And what about Julie? What had happened to her?

In the end, a man just has to put all his questions and doubts aside and do what has to be done. That's what it all came down to that day on the bench below the sliderock slope. I set my feet, took a deep breath, and readied my lasso. With a quick whirl, I tossed my loop up toward the nubbin. The rope struck the face of the hill, two feet short of the rock. The lariat fell back down about me, its coils clattering against the ledge. I took a moment to steady myself and tried to clear my mind of questions and fear. Twice, three times more, I tried the throw. Each time the loop went wide of the mark or fell short.

I coiled the rope again, concentrating on the job at hand. I focused my attention on that jutting stone above me. I pictured the loop climbing against gravity, going up and settling cleanly over the rock. When the picture was clear in my mind, I threw my lariat up with all my strength, turned my wrist to open the loop—and made the catch!

Even then, my troubles were not over. Would the rock hold? Would it bear my weight? Decisions come easy when there's only one choice a man can make. Grasping the rope in both hands, I leaned back until it was taut. Then, my feet walking up the incline, I pulled myself hand over hand toward the top. Moments later, I reached the crest and sprawled full length among the rocks beside the trail.

Rutherford whinnied when he saw me. The little buckskin stood ground-tied where I'd left him near the stump. A gust of wind tossed his mane and tail and stirred the grass alongside the trail. I walked over to him on shaky legs and hugged his neck. Turning away, I scanned the hilltop. The vista reached out and away, the trail leading down the spine of the crest to the valley beyond the canyon. There was grass, blowing in the wind. There was rock, and red rock, and patches of cedar and sage. There was Rutherford and me and that same hawk riding the air currents. But there was no black mare, no tracks on the rocky trail, and there was no Julie McAllister. Not anywhere.

Back at the spring, Hoodoo sat with his back against the bedroll and watched me ride up. His rifle was across his knees, and his face looked haggard and drawn. "About time you got here," he said. "Where's the girl?"

I stepped down off Rutherford and shook my head. "It's a long story," I said, "but it ends with 'she's gone'."

"I can't wait to hear it," Hoodoo said, "but I've got news of my own. We had us a visitor a while back."

Something in way he said "visitor" caught my attention. I glanced around the camp and saw the horses grazing—Hoodoo's paint, the bay horse and the gray I'd bought from Keppler, and the white packhorse. Then I saw the other horse.

"That's the little cayuse Keppler's man rides," I said. "Was he here?"

"Still is," said Hoodoo. "That would be him over yonder, under the tarp. He was a mite hostile earlier, but he's plum peaceful now."

I followed his glance to the cottonwood log where our packsaddles and tack were stacked. The canvas sheet we used as a manty on our packhorse lay spread on the ground, held down by rocks. I could see by the mounded shape at its center that it covered something, but it was the boots sticking out from underneath that told me what that something was. Still attached to the boots were the cruel Spanish spurs he had worn and used so freely. I looked at Hoodoo. "Rafael?" I asked. "He's dead?"

"He was when I covered him up. I expect he still is."

"Are you going to tell me what happened, or should I just keep asking questions so you can make smart remarks?"

Hoodoo shrugged. "It was that tinhorn bankroll of yours. I was feelin' poorly after you and the girl rode out, but not so bad I didn't notice Rafael coyoting around out yonder on the flat.

"I was laying here in my blankets when he rode in. He drawed rein and stepped down without being invited. Then he looked all around like a wolf smelling a trap. 'Where is your *companero?*' he asks, 'Where is the deputy?'

"Like I said, I was feelin' poorly. Sweatin' like a field hand. Shakin' like leaves on a quakin' asp. I said you were close by, but he didn't believe me. He said, 'I don' think so. I don' see that buckskin he rides.' Then he walked over to our packs and commenced to paw through our plunder, keeping an eye on me all the while.

"He said, 'I think that deputy owes me some money. That deputy's got a big bankroll.'

"Then he got bolder. He poured himself a cup of coffee and walked over toward me. 'What's the

158

matter with you?' he asks, 'You *enfermo?* You sick?'

"He looked around again, then looked back at me. 'I think maybe I'll take some of your things, hombre. Maybe I'll take your horses."

Then he pulled his pistol and came over here to where I was laying. He said, 'What you got under that old blanket, anyway?'

"What I had under the blanket was my .45 Colt's Peacemaker. I touched it off just as he bent over me. Bullet put a hole in the blanket and set it on fire, but Rafael never smelled the smoke."

I walked over and lifted up a corner of the tarp. The body lay on its side roughly in the shape of an "L." Hoodoo's bullet had struck Rafael dead center in his forehead. "Well," I said, "I lost the girl today and spent an hour or so trapped on a mountain ledge. I suppose it's just as well we had a shooting to round out the day."

Hoodoo closed his eyes and lay back. "For what it's worth, I didn't particularly want to kill him. That's just the way it worked out."

"Self-defense," I said, "but it does complicate things. We'll have to take the body in and make a report. Maybe go back to Fort Savage."

Hoodoo nodded. "Sorry, kid," he said. "Sorry about the girl, too."

"Yeah," I said, "so am I."

I made a fresh pot of coffee and warmed up the beans and bacon. I told Hoodoo to help himself to the whiskey if we still had any, but he declined with a shake of his head. As we ate, I told him of the events of the morning. I recounted my ride with Julie to the hill above the canyon. I told him how I'd dropped her book at the edge of the trail. I described my descent to the ledge to fetch it back, and how I wound up stranded. I told him of hearing Julie call my name, and of my calling out to her. Finally, I told him how I'd roped the rock nubbin and climbed back up to the top of the hill. There had been no sign of Julie, her horse, or of anyone else, I told him. "I'm not the tracker you are," I said, "but I wasn't able to pick up any fresh tracks, either."

I finished the last of my supper and set the plate down. "I feel like a dern fool," I told him, "but I'm not sure what I could have done different."

"A man can always find a way to blame himself," Hoodoo said.

"We had her back, and I lost her. Who else should I blame?"

Hoodoo sipped his coffee in silence. I stood, looking out toward where the horses grazed in the late light. I turned back to Hoodoo. "You didn't see anyone beside Rafael come through today, did you?"

Hoodoo finished his coffee and set the cup down on the ground. "There was one thing, maybe an hour after you two rode out." He pointed toward a red-rock butte west of camp. "I saw light flashes from up there. Sunlight flashing off a mirror, likely. Could have been Indians, or maybe soldiers from the fort using a Heliograph. Sort of like Morse Code, it was— three longs, then a stop. Then three more."

Hoodoo fell silent, remembering. Then he said, "That's all I saw, until Rafael showed up. No riders, no men on foot."

I stood, tossing the coffee grounds out of my cup. "I think I'll bring the horses closer in before it gets dark," I said. "Maybe we can pick up some tracks in the morning."

Hoodoo coughed and closed his eyes. "Maybe," he said, "but if them boys came and took the girl again they'll have quite a lead on us. I ain't sure I'm up to the chase."

I nodded. "I reckon it's time to fall back and regroup. This trail has gone cold. Tomorrow, we'll take Rafael's carcass back to Fort Savage and telegraph Ridgeway."

"We should make quite a procession, riding in to the fort."

"You bet," I said, "a dead thief, a crippled scout, and a failed deputy marshal."

I took the horses to water and set them to graze while Hoodoo washed the dishes. I could see his leg was hurting him considerable, though he never complained or let on by any direct sign. He had made himself a kind of crutch from a cottonwood branch, and I was surprised—and pleased—to see how well he was able to get around.

· · ·

We sat near the fire for awhile after supper, but neither of us was much in a mood for palaver. As for me, I was baffled and low in my mind because of losing Julie again. Hoodoo was still sitting by the fire when I turned in, his features lit by the glow of the dying coals.

Sleeping out under the stars always seemed to lift my spirits. I liked to lie on my back and watch the dark skies come alive with stars beyond the counting, and feel the cares of the day fall away. As I watched the night sky, the feeling would come over me that something bigger than me and my puny efforts was in charge. I would tell myself I could turn loose of my worries and drop off to a deep and peaceful slumber. I had done my best, I'd tell myself, and the results weren't up to me.

But this time that feeling didn't come. I laid awake a long while, thinking about the events of the day, but I could find no meaning nor hope in my ponderings. I tried to tell myself I had done my best, but the telling didn't help. If I had done my best, it had not been good enough. Julie was missing once again. I had no idea where she'd gone or how to get her back. My mind was filled with random and scattered notions, but there was no clear picture of what I should do. The stars came out in their old, familiar glory, but I took no pleasure in them. Thoughts of Julie crowded my mind until at last I fell asleep, but even then I dreamed of her.

I was up, if not awake, before first light. Hoodoo already had breakfast well begun when I stumbled up to the fire. He handed me a steaming cup of coffee and said, "This will burn away the cobwebs and get your heart started." I took the cup in both hands and set down cross-legged beside him. I admired his cheerfulness, but I couldn't match it. I generally wake up some hours later than I get up, and I am not at my best until well past sunrise. I nodded my thanks and took a sip. The coffee was strong, hot, and welcome. "I put a spoon of black-strap in there," Hoodoo said, "so she's black as night and sweet as love."

Fried taters and bacon simmered on the fire, and Hoodoo ladled us each a plateful. After adding a piece each of fry bread from a skillet, we hunkered down and commenced to break the fast. I looked at Hoodoo, and found to my surprise that I had come to like him. He was sarcastic, ofttimes contrary, and usually cantankerous, but he had been there for me when the chips were down. He had borne his wound without complaint, and he had—for the present, at least—put aside his craving for whiskey.

"How's your leg wound this mornin'?" I asked.

"Just fine!" says he. "Everyone should have one!"

"I'm serious. How is it? Can you ride?"

Hoodoo slid his plate and eating tools into the dish-water. "I will, whether I can or not," he said. "Yeah. I can ride."

"I'll need your help packing our outfit. Figured we can pack your victim on his own horse."

"We could leave him for the coyotes, and not pack him at all."

"He's your trophy. I figured you'd probably want to take him to a taxidermist."

Hoodoo added my plate to the dishwater. "Go ahead, have your fun," he said, "but I'll have the last laugh if there's a reward out for that bird."

A bright spot burned on the rim of the eastern mountains. A moment later, sunlight exploded across the valley.

I stood up and high-heeled it toward the horses. "Well," said I, "another day, another dollar."

With Hoodoo's help, I packed the panniers and bedroll on the packhorse and tied the load down with a one-man diamond hitch. Then I turned to the matter of the dead thief. The late, unlamented Rafael had met his end maybe sixteen hours earlier. I figured his corpse would still be stiff as a board, and therefore something of a challenge to pack on a horse.

Old Ambrose, proprietor of the funeral parlor back in Dry Creek, had once told me that rigor mortis generally sets in from five minutes to several hours after death, and that it lasts about twenty-four hours after that. My best guess was that Rafael had turned up his toes no more than eighteen hours earlier. So it was with some concern that I approached the tarp that covered his body and lifted it off.

I was relieved to find that once again Hoodoo Hawks had anticipated the problem and had taken steps to solve it. As I had noted the day before, Hoodoo had laid the thief on his side in an "L" shape before he covered him.

I'd like to believe the little cayuse was glad Rafael had gone to his great reward, but if so, the animal did not seem all that eager to carry its tormentor's carcass on its last ride. Even after we blindfolded the horse, it trembled and fidgeted something awful before we were able to get the body lashed down for the trip. We jackknifed Rafael over his riding saddle, tied his wrists and ankles to opposite stirrups, and then tied the stirrups together.

All told, packing Rafael's corpse was the most difficult part of breaking camp. It delayed our departure some, but at least it provided me with the opportunity to chide Hoodoo for causing so much trouble by shooting the rascal in the first place.

I helped Hoodoo mount his paint horse and gave him the lead rope to the packhorse and the horses I'd bought from Keppler. Then I took the little horse's bridle reins and led out with the dead Rafael in tow. I turned in the saddle, looking back. Hoodoo was right. We made quite a procession.

We rode east, into the rising sun, back toward Fort Savage. It was hard for me to turn back. Although I had no idea where Julie was, I had the strange feeling we were somehow riding away from her. I kept looking back over my shoulder, as if she might suddenly appear behind us. I can't explain my feelings, except to say I felt I was giving up the search. Worse than that, I felt I was giving up on Julie.

I told Hoodoo I intended to stop at Keppler's ranch on the way to inform him of Rafael's death and ask a few questions regarding the man's criminal activities. I don't know what I expected to accomplish, but I figured it was what Ridgeway would have done.

We had crossed Curlew Creek and were perhaps two miles from Keppler's when we met a cavalry patrol from Fort Savage. The patrol was a small force—only fifteen men—but it was commanded by Major Burdette himself. It also included a prisoner, seated on his horse with his hands tied behind him— the rancher, George Keppler!

Major Burdette rode at the column's head beside a long-haired scout in buckskins. The scout pointed at Hoodoo and me, and Burdette ordered the column to halt. Leaving the troopers in place, Burdette and the scout rode out to meet us. Hoodoo and me drew rein, waiting for them.

The major seemed uncomfortable in the field. His face was flushed, and dust powdered his blue flannel army blouse. As he approached, he removed his hat, mopping his brow with a bandanna. I had the feeling he couldn't wait to get back to his bath at Fort Savage.

Burdette and the scout reined up, their eyes taking in both our horses and the cayuse with its mortal burden. "Good morning, Deputy," Burdette said. "I see you acquired the horses you needed."

"Morning, Major," I said. "We haven't had occasion to use them yet. I followed your advice and bought the bay and the gray from George Keppler."

Major Burdette nodded. Beside me, Hoodoo and the scout traded glances. I figured they knew each other. It struck me as queer, the way neither they nor we were saying what was on our minds. I know they were wondering about Rafael's body, draped beneath the canvas on his nervous little horse. For our part, we had noticed that George Keppler was obviously in army custody, which sure aroused my curiosity. It was like there was some kind of unwritten rule that nobody could ask a question until the other feller brought the subject up. I decided to outwait them.

"You may have noticed," the major began, "that Mr. Keppler is our unwilling guest. Two nights ago, five army horses were stolen from the pasture outside the fort. There were conflicting stories by witnesses. One said the animals were taken by Indians. Another identified the bandit as one Rafael Chavez, hired hand of George Keppler. I organized a patrol to investigate, and to retrieve the army mounts.

"We found all five missing horses this morning in Keppler's pasture. The brands had been altered. Mr. Keppler has no explanation as to how the horses came to be in his possession."

The major paused. He glanced again at Rafael's body. "We were on our way to offer Mr. Chavez our hospitality, as well. We have a few questions for him."

"I'm afraid Mr. Chavez may be short on answers," I said. "That's him beneath the canvas yonder. He passed away sudden-like while attempting to rob our camp."

The major nodded at the corpse, then looked back at me. "May I?" he asked.

"Please," I said.

Burdette dismounted, handing his reins to the long-haired scout. He walked to the little cayuse, folded back the canvas, and lifted Rafael's head up by its hair. "Yes, that's Mr. Chavez, all right," he said. The big .45-caliber hole in Rafael's forehead was an ugly sight. "I believe I just may have discovered the cause of his death," Burdette said wryly.

The major was about to mount his horse again when he paused, looking up at me. "Did you find the two men and the woman you were looking for?" he asked.

"That's kind of a long story, Major," I said.

"The reason I ask is one of our patrols came in late last night. Those soldiers had also been looking for missing army horses."

Burdette swung up into the saddle with a grunt. He took the reins from his scout. "Didn't find the horses," he said, "but they did observe riders just before sundown. There were two men and a woman."

twelve

If we had been playing poker, Major Burdette could have taken everything I owned. When he said "two men and a woman" I sat up straight in my saddle and nearly fell off my horse. It was a moment or two before I could speak. Then, trying to sound casual, I said, "Two men and a woman? Uh—did your men say where they saw these folks?"

"Northeast of the fort, maybe ten miles," Burdette said. "In the badlands between Little Woody and Big Woody Creeks."

The location was all wrong. The badlands were a good thirty miles from where Julie disappeared! If the kidnappers had taken her again, they couldn't have made it that far, not so soon. It wasn't possible—or was it?

"I don't believe they could be the people we're after," I said. "Did your troopers describe them?"

"They only saw them for a moment. The three came out of one coulee, riding hard, and dropped back into another. My men were looking into the setting sun."

I turned the news over in my mind. I knew the country Burdette spoke of. I had hunted mustangs there with my pa when I was just a button. The badland country was a place of sun-blasted hills, dry, rocky gulches, and box canyons. It was wild country, shunned by all—all, that is, except badmen on the run and the occasional Indian.

I looked at Hoodoo. He saw the question in my eyes. Could he make it? I recalled his words back at the spring when I asked him if he could ride:

"I will, whether I can or not. Yeah, I can ride." Still looking at him, I raised an eyebrow. Hoodoo nodded.

I turned back to the major. "Is the telegraph from Fort Savage still open? I sure would like to report to Marshal Ridgeway."

Major Burdette looked rueful. "Sorry, Deputy. The line went down the day after you left the fort. I haven't had the time or the manpower to look for the break."

"Can I ask you a favor, Major?"

"Of course."

"Well, if Hoodoo and me did decide to head over into the breaks, we'd need to travel fast and light. I'd like to leave the packhorse and the late Mr. Chavez in your custody."

It was Burdette's turn to think things over. After a moment, he said, "I think we can accommodate you, Deputy, on one condition."

"What's that?"

"If you run across any loose army horses, bring them back when you come. We're wearing out the ones we have, trying to find the ones we *haven't*."

I laughed. "Done," I said.

When the troopers had moved off with Rafael and our packhorse, Hoodoo and me took inventory. I had appropriated Rafael's saddlebags to replace the ones the kidnappers took at Alkali Springs. We tied blanket rolls behind the cantles of our saddles. The troopers gave us some of their hardtack to sustain us on the trail, although we didn't have a sledge hammer to break it up. Army hardtack has to be the hardest substance knowed to man. I believe they could use it to cut diamonds.

We had laid in a store of coffee, salt, and jerked beef from our pack and replenished our ammunition supply. My Henry rifle and my six-gun fired the same .44 cartridge. I filled the loops of my gunbelt and put the rest of the bullets in my saddle pockets.

Hoodoo had two full boxes of .45 cartridges for his Colt's Peacemaker and a box of .45-70s for his Sharps rifle. I put my saddle on the gray horse I'd bought from Keppler and cinched Hoodoo's hull on the bay. We filled our canteens at Curlew Creek, took the lead ropes for Rutherford and the paint, and struck out at a lope, our sights set on the badlands.

Because it was the first time I had rode the gray, I paid particular attention to its behavior. The gray was a strong horse, tough and blocky, and I knew he could carry the mail. But there was something of the ambusher about him, which caused me concern. Most horses will buck some at first saddle of a morning, especially when the weather is frosty. They do so out of high spirits, I reckon, and because they're feeling frisky. There's no meanness in such horses. They just need to warp their backbones a little to celebrate the day. Afterward, they settle down to a hard day's work, remaining on their best behavior until quitting time. That's *most* horses.

There are other horses who seldom buck in the morning but save their insurrections for later in the day. They'll plod along, peaceful as doves and gentle as lambs, but war is in their hearts. Just when a man is deep in the timber, or pushing steers down a slope, such a horse will blow up like a powder keg and cause his rider to take up a homestead. I was beginning to suspect the gray was one of that breed. In any case, I resolved to keep a watchful eye on the horse, at least until we were better acquainted.

Hoodoo and me kept our pace until midday, alternating the horses between a run and a fast trot. Just past noon, we came onto a brushy grove near a clear-running stream, and I decided we'd shade up there and rest the horses. Hoodoo said I needn't stop on his account. When I asked him about his leg, he said it didn't hurt, but I knowed he sometimes lied about other things, too. I said I didn't care whether his dern leg hurt or not. I told him the gray horse had a bone-jarring sop-and-taters trot and that it was *me* who needed rest. I don't know if he believed me, but at least he pretended to.

We ate some jerked beef, and I soaked a piece of the army hardtack in creek water until I could break off a chunk here and there. Then I found a grassy spot under a chokecherry tree and took a twenty-minute snooze. Hoodoo said he wasn't tired, but when I came to, he was on his back in the sunshine, his snoring like the sound of a sawmill in full swing. I drug him into the shade and let him sleep maybe a half hour longer before I woke him.

"Time to move out, Hoodoo," I said.

He was instantly awake. His faded blue eyes focused on me. He rolled onto his side, and sat up. His voice was terse when he spoke. "Let's ride then," he said. "You ain't waitin' on me."

We had tied the horses to green branches inside the grove and had loosened the girths of the bay and the gray. Now that the animals had cooled out some, I allowed them each a drink at the creek, then tightened their cinches again. Watching Hoodoo out of the corner of my eye, it seemed to me he was still in considerable pain. His face was tight, and he moved with a careful concentration that spoke truer than his words.

"We'll need to slow up a mite," he said. "Keep an eye out for tracks. Them folks may have followed a game path, or rode the ridges. Somewhere out there, we'll cut their trail."

"And then?"

Hoodoo's face showed strain, the muscles in his jaw hard and knotted. "And then," he said, "we'll follow along until the tracks end. Right there, at that very spot, I expect we'll find our people standin' in 'em."

By two o'clock in the afternoon we had entered the edge of the badlands. There, in late summer, the scant grass had turned tawny as cougar hair, and the twisted sagebrush had gone from healthy green to faded olive. Under a cloudless sky the rock-strewn ridges and slopes shimmered red, yellow, and brown in the sunlight. The air was stifling, as hard to breathe as water. Sweat trickled down my face, stinging my eyes and blurring my vision.

My thoughts began to drift. I thought again of Julie and our ride together the day she disappeared. I remembered her expression, happy and excited as a child. She had talked about her poetry book—her favorite, she'd said. She had handed it to me. Then our hands had collided. I recalled fumbling, somehow dropping the book over the edge of the slope, its pages fluttering like the wings of a falling bird. I remembered my climb down to retrieve it, leaning back against the tension of the rope, my feet walking me down the face of the hill.

And then, as I picked up the book, I saw the rope I had secured to the stump above falling to the narrow ledge where I stood. It had not broken, nor had it been cut. It had simply been loosened from the stump where I'd tied it and allowed to fall. Julie had called my name from above, her voice sounding frightened and sad somehow. Then she was gone. What had happened up there? Where was Julie? I tried to think, but I could make no sense of the facts as I knew them.

Ahead of me, Hoodoo hobbled slowly along a game trail atop a low hill, leading his horse. From time to time, he'd stop, studying the ground before him. I dismounted and followed him on foot, leading the gray, as well as Rutherford and the paint. Sunlight bore down on my shoulders, heavy as lead and hot as a brand. Time seemed to stop. The sun glared down. I felt drowsy, dull, and listless.

"We've got company."

Hoodoo stood stock still in the trail, his head high and his eyes fixed on the distance. I looked in the direction of his gaze and saw a single tepee, standing across the valley in a thicket beside a slow-moving stream. The lodge was a sort of gray white in color, except for its top. The tepee's top had been painted a deep red.

Near the tepee, two paint horses and a sorrel stood beside the stream. They had stopped grazing and stood staring across the valley at us. An old Indian man came out of the lodge, shaded his eyes, and followed the horses' gaze.

"Old friend of mine," Hoodoo said. "Crow medicine man name of Bear-that-sings. His is the only lodge in the Crow nation painted that way."

"What's he doing here?" I asked. "This don't seem like the best place to set up camp."

"Let's pay him a visit," Hoodoo said. "You can ask him. He just might invite us to supper."

"I thought the idea was to move fast." I said. "We need to pick up the trail of the people we're after."

"No argument there, Deputy. Trouble is, we *haven't* picked up their trail. If anyone came through this country lately, I expect old Bear-that-sings will know it."

"Do you savvy the Crow language?" I asked. "*I* sure don't."

"Some. And I savvy sign language pretty well."

"Lead on then," I told him. "You're the scout for this outfit."

Hoodoo turned his horse so he could mount the animal from the uphill side. He tried to hide the hurt his leg caused him, but I could see it in his face. He sat unmoving for a moment, then reined the horse about and led the way down to the valley floor. I swung up on the gray and followed.

Bear-that-sings stood in front of his lodge, wearing nothing but his breechcloth and a bear-claw necklace. His long hair was silver gray, and he wore it in three long braids, after the manner of the Crow. Old scars marked his sagging chest muscles where the pegs had torn his flesh at some long-ago Sun Dance. What few teeth he had left were scattered at random in his mouth, and he showed them all when he recognized Hoodoo. Wrinkles rippled across his leathery face with the fullness of his smile. His voice was quavery and high-pitched when he spoke, and his laugh was a giggle that made a feller laugh just to hear it.

"Hoo-doo!" he cackled. "HOO-DOO! AH-HO!" He spoke rapidly, his words interrupted from time to time by that high-pitched giggle. There was no need for a translator; Bear-that-sings was welcoming us to his home.

Hoodoo slid out of the saddle and shook hands with the old medicine man. Bear-that-sings gripped his friend's arm with his left hand while he shook hands with his right. Hoodoo said something in the Crow tongue, grinning almost as wide as he had while talking to Julie. The two men carried on like that for awhile, and then Hoodoo introduced me.

"MER-LIN FAN-SHAW," Hoodoo said. Then pointing to himself, he said, "My part-ner. PART-NE

Bear-that-sings sized me up with one quick glance, grinning and nodding his head. We shook hands, and then the old man reached out and touched the deputy's badge that was pinned to my shirt. "SIL-ver Star," he said. "SIL-VER Star! AH-HO!"

Hoodoo chuckled. "Seems Bear-that-sings don't like your name all that much. He just gave you another'n, Silver Star."

I grinned. "One name is as good as another, I suppose. How do I tell him 'thank you'?"

"Ah-ho' will do. Means 'much obliged' and 'welcome' both, I understand."

I told the old man "Ah-ho" and led the horses out a little way from the lodge to tie them inside the thicket. Bear-that-sings and Hoodoo hunkered down together in front of the tepee, conversing in the Crow tongue and sign language. I had just finished with the horses when I saw Bear-that-sings's woman come into camp. She carried a brace of prairie chickens and a short club of hardwood. She was a comely woman, maybe half Bear-Singer's age. She smiled shyly as she saw me and carried the birds off behind the lodge—to pluck them, I suppose.

If anything, it was even hotter there in the valley than it had been atop the hill. The thicket provided some shade, and the stream that ran past their tepee made it seem cooler, even if it wasn't. The stakes that pegged the tepee's cover to the ground had been pulled up, and the cover raised around the bottom to take advantage of whatever breeze there might be. Bear-that-sings's lodge cover was made of sewn canvas. With the once great buffalo herds growing fewer and maybe gone forever, the old buffalo-hide lodges were becoming rare.

Hoodoo and Bear-that-sings were still deep in conversation, with many a gesture and sign. I set down beside them, not understanding a single word. I smiled, and did my best to appear intelligent. When they would laugh, I'd laugh. When they'd pause and look thoughtful, so would I. And when they'd look my way, I'd nod my head as if to say I agreed with them, even though I had no idea what I was agreeing to.

Finally, I got to feeling so foolish I stood up and wandered back down to where the horses were. At first, I was afraid I might have broke some serious rule of Indian etiquette and that the entire Crow tribe would have a warrant out on me for rudeness, but as it turned out I don't think Hoodoo and Bear even noticed I'd gone.

Missus Bear-that-sings had fried up those prairie chickens at a small cookfire out back of the lodge and had cooked up a batch of something that looked like wild turnips to go with it. I suppose she did her cooking outside to keep from heating up the lodge. She gave me a big smile, and said something pleasant-sounding in Crow. I tipped my hat and said, "Yes, ma'am. Thank you, ma'am." I know she didn't understand a word I said, but it sure made her giggle. Must have been the way I said it.

The shadows grew long, and the sky took on some color. Hoodoo came limping toward me in that stiff, held-together way people use when they're trying to hide their pain.

"I'm glad the powwow ended before bedtime," I grumped. "I'd ask you what he said, except I don't think I have time to wait for the full translation."

Hoodoo grinned. "I couldn't tell you, anyway," he said. "I only savvied maybe a third of it myself."

"What are him and his wife doin' out here all alone?" I asked.

"They come here every year. Seems they gather some kind of special root he uses in his medicine man business. Says it only grows here in the badlands."

"If he's a medicine man, maybe you ought to let him look at your leg."

"Maybe you ought to mind your own business."

"I figure keepin' my tracker fit *is* my business."

179

"Let it go, kid."

I shrugged. "All right," I said. "What else did he say?"

Hoodoo eased himself down beside the stream and commenced to wash his face and hands. "Well, he asked us to supper. Said we should stay the night."

"Neighborly of him, but we've got outlaws to find."

Hoodoo raised his head and looked out toward the setting sun. After a long moment he said, "Suppose I tell you they're already found?"

He had my full attention. "*Is* that what you're telling me?"

"Bear-that-sings claims he saw them come through yesterday. Two men and a woman. Says he knows where they're camped."

I could hardly breathe. "Where?"

"In a canyon maybe five miles west of here. Holed up in an old trapper's cabin. Bear-that-sings followed them."

"Two men and a woman? You think he really saw Julie?"

"I pushed him on that. I asked him, 'Was the woman young and pretty?' He thought about the question for a moment, then broke out laughing. 'No,' he says. 'She was a white woman!' Then he laughed even harder."

"Some joke," I said. "All right, let's ride."

Hoodoo shook his head. "Think about it, Deputy. It'll be full dark soon. If we try to take them boys tonight, they might slip away again."

I thought about it. "Maybe you're right," I said. "If we were to be at the cabin at first light tomorrow we could pretty well *surround* those fellers."

Hoodoo grinned. "I like your spirit, kid," he said. "It ain't all that easy for two men to *make* a surround."

We dined with Mr. and Mrs. Bear-that-sings that evening. I guess her cooking was just fine—Hoodoo seemed to think so. As for me, I couldn't even tell you what I ate, let alone if it was good or not. All I could think of was that I had another chance to rescue Julie. I kept going over my plans for the morning. I tried to imagine what the canyon would be like, how the cabin would lay, where the outlaw's horses would be. I promised myself we'd rescue Julie for sure this time and get her daddy's money back besides. As for the kidnappers, we'd take them in just the way it says on the posters—dead or alive.

After supper, we said our thank-yous and rolled out our blankets down by the creek. The stars seemed close enough to touch and bright enough to keep a man from sleeping, but it wasn't the stars that kept me awake. It was the memory of Julie's soft voice and the way her eyes drawed a person in and held him. We could not—*would* not—fail this time. The Almighty had gave me a second chance, and I aimed to make it good.

181

thirteen

The big dipper had finished its nightly roll around the north star and stood level just above the horizon. I had slept but little during the night, dozing and waking in fits and starts as I thought of what might await us in the morning. The night had been cool. I had lain awake for much of it, listening to the night sounds—the rippling of the stream beside us, the shuffling of our horses. I had mostly thought of Julie. Finding her occupied my thoughts and filled my dreams. I knew that Hoodoo and me would no doubt be going up against desperate men, yet I had no fear. Saving Julie and getting her safely back to her father was what busied my mind.

The yip and yodel of a coyote—or more than one; it's hard to tell with coyotes—came from somewhere out in the dark. The cry seemed both close and far away, and I couldn't tell whether another bunch of song-dogs had answered the first or if the echo was due to coyote ventriloquism.

I sat up and put my hat on. Hoodoo slept nearby, his breathing steady and deep. He had slept fitfully during the night, first shivering beneath his blankets, then casting them off as if he was running a fever. From time to time he had murmured in his sleep, but I wasn't able to make out the words.

False dawn brought light to the land. I figured the time to be about four. I turned my boots over and shook them to get rid of any critters that may have took up residence there, then pulled them on. It had been hot the day before, and would be again this day, but the morning was cool if not downright cold. I put on my vest and buttoned it, waiting for my body to get used to the chill. Leaving Hoodoo to sleep a few minutes more, I rolled my blankets and made my way to the horses.

Rutherford nickered softly as I walked up to him. He seemed rested, and I saw he had put on some flesh since I'd been riding the gray. For a moment, I thought about taking him on the raid, but in the end I chose the gray again. I would give Rutherford another day's rest.

I watered our horses and put the hobbles back on Rutherford and Hoodoo's paint. Then I saddled the gray and the bay horse and led them back to where we'd slept. The Indian horses were dark shapes in the gloom, but I recalled from the day before they seemed old and in poor condition. It appeared that Bear-that-sings owned three horses—one for him, one for his missus, and one to drag the lodge poles and carry the tepee. I decided I liked the old Indian. He was poor as Job's turkey, but he was generous and full of humor all the same.

Hoodoo was awake and dressed when I brought the horses up. I was no tracker—not the way he was—but I had rode with him long enough to read his signs. He stood hunched in the dark beside the stream, and I could tell he was in real pain.

"Before you play nurse Nellie and ask me again if I can ride," he growled, "the answer is hell yes I can ride. Just get me on my horse."

"You're no good to me if you're sick," I told him. "I can do the job without you."

"Maybe. But we'll never know for sure, because you ain't goin' without me."

I gave him a leg up onto his horse. "You're about half stubborn," I said. "You know that?"

"More than half," he said.

Hoodoo led the way, following the map he had made in his head. He rode through the darkness as if it was light, going west into the rough country that had no name but badlands. Up narrow trails we went, down through dry washes, horses laboring on the inclines and sliding on shale and slide rock going down. I twisted in the saddle, looking back. In the east the sun was coming, lightening the sky, chasing the stars away. Five miles, Hoodoo had said. How far had we come? How much farther did we have to go?

Sunlight broke behind us, painting the hilltops and making the canyons seem darker still. Ahead, Hoodoo drew rein and sat huddled in the saddle, waiting for me to ride up. When I reached him, he whispered, "The cabin is just over that next rise. I smelled woodsmoke a mile back. Help me down, and we'll slip up and take a look."

The cabin was a gray shape in the gloom. It backed up against a rocky slope that was studded with jack-pine and juniper. Smoke drifted from a rusted chimney and disappeared into the morning. "Cookin' breakfast," Hoodoo whispered.

The canyon was like a dozen I'd seen, hunting mustangs with Pa. Up from the cabin, half-hidden by twisted pines and fallen rock, was an old corral, its logs silver with age. It was a round corral, built for working mustangs, and there were horses inside. I looked for Julie's black mare, but didn't see her. I couldn't really make out any of the horses clearly, but I could see there were some inside the corral.

Like the door of Bear-that-sings's tepee, the cabin door faced east, into the rising sun. There was one window, to the right of the door. An old wagon road, overgrown with weeds, climbed the hill we lay upon and dropped down to the cabin. I motioned Hoodoo to follow me and backed away from the hilltop on my belly.

Once we were out of sight I laid out our plan of attack. Hoodoo would take up a vantage point where he could see the cabin and corral, covering the area with his Sharps buffalo gun. I would enter the canyon on horseback at its lower end, blocking the outlaws' escape. If they made a dash for the horses and tried to escape by way of the canyon's upper end Hoodoo would have an open field of fire with the Sharps. I thought the plan a good one, and it was. It just didn't happen to work out anything *like* the way I expected.

As sunlight spread into the canyon, I rode the gray down the slope and turned him up toward the cabin. I carried my Henry rifle across the forks of my saddle, and I couldn't help wondering who might be watching me from the window.

It's funny how the mind works. As I approached the cabin, everything seemed to slow down to a snail's pace. The horse's steps seemed to bring us no closer, or only barely so. Sound seemed to slow down, too. I heard a meadowlark somewhere off to my left, but its song dragged like music played on a gramophone that wanted winding.

At the same time, my eyesight seemed to grow sharper. I could clearly see the wood grain on the cabin now, from seventy yards away. I saw the rust on the door hinges, the chipped wash basin on a bench outside, the woodsmoke's slow rise to catch pink light above the shadow of the hill.

Then, fifty yards away, the cabin door swung open and a woman stepped out. She carried a slop jar, and she turned away, not seeing me, to empty the pail behind the cabin. Returning, she turned to reenter the cabin, and saw me. I reined up, and for what seemed a long time, we just looked at each other. She was a big-boned and buxom woman, maybe thirty-five or so. She wore a short riding coat over a man's work shirt and rough woolen britches. Her hair was long, black, and tangled as a magpie's nest. You could not have called her pretty.

I touched my hat brim and said, "Good morning, ma'am. My name is Merlin Fanshaw, and I'm a deputy United States marshal. I need to ask you a few questions, if I may."

For a moment she just stood, staring. Then she dropped the bucket, drawing a pistol from her coat as she sprang for the door. "Lawdogs, Vince!" she yelled and fired at me point blank!

I felt the bullet brush past as I reined the gray sharply to one side, spurring him away from danger purely by instinct. It was at that moment the gray chose to go to bucking, and in the next half-second I lost my hat, my Henry rifle, and my sunny disposition.

The woman was walking toward me, holding the pistol with both hands and firing at me as fast as she could cock the piece and pull the trigger.

I remember thinking, "That lady is really trying to kill me!" Behind her, a big man stepped quickly out of the cabin and commenced to shoot at me with a Winchester!

I had expected the gray would blow up with me at the worst possible time, and he did not disappoint me. He bucked across the way, popping his back and driving his feet down hard into the dirt. Then he swapped ends and bucked back the other way, squealing like a boar hog and chopping up turf, while the man and the woman kept firing as if I was a duck in a shooting gallery.

The gray had surprised me, right enough, but he

was a long way from unloading me. I took a deep seat and clung to the saddle like a burr to a blanket. While being shot at was far from pleasant, it was not at the moment my chief concern. Who the shooters were was a mystery to me, but with the gray horse buck-jumping like he was I figured they'd have to be better shots than Bill Hickok to do me any damage.

In all the excitement, it had temporarily slipped my mind that a horse was bigger than a man, and there-fore more likely to be struck by a bullet. Suddenly, the gray squealed and went down head first. Bright blood sprayed from his neck and withers as I kicked loose of the stirrups and stepped off. The gray was down, his powerful back legs jerking in air. Crouched behind the struggling animal, I brought my .44 to bear and began to return fire.

A second man, as big as the first, had dashed out of the cabin. He held a shotgun in his hands and seemed intent on getting close enough to use it. It was then I heard the roar of Hoodoo's buffalo gun and saw the second man slammed back through the cabin door. Hoodoo fired again, gouging up a geyser of dirt just in front of the woman. Both she and the first man let up on their shooting, looking toward the hilltop in an effort to see where the gunfire was coming from. The woman turned, running back inside the cabin. The man was turning his attention back to me when I took advantage of Hoodoo's diversion and put him down with a well-placed revolver shot.

The big man dropped his Winchester when my bullet struck him. Moving quickly, I crossed the distance between us and reached him just as he was trying to pick it up again. I put a boot on his chest and pushed him back to the ground. "Let it alone," I warned him. "The fight's over."

Close-up, the man was even bigger. He showed his teeth and scowled, looking at me with a glare that seemed to say, "It's not over until I quit."

His hand was almost on the rifle when I kicked it out of reach. I cocked the .44 and offered him a look into its barrel. "Give it up," I said. "I don't want to kill you."

The big man rolled over and sat up. "Well, I sure as hell don't want to be killed," he said. "You win, lawdog."

"Tell the woman to come out," I said, "with her hands up."

He grunted, clutching his belly where my bullet had struck him. When he took his hand away, it was red with blood. He twisted his body back toward the cabin. "Ramona! Lawdog wants you out here—with your hands up, he says."

Hesitantly, the woman came outside and into the sunlight. She held her hands above her head as she walked toward me. "Cletus is dead," she announced. The big man's expression didn't change, but I saw his jaw tighten briefly, then relax. "Had to happen sometime," he said.

Behind me, the gray horse lay in the bloody dust,

still kicking. The outlaw frowned. "You gonna shoot that horse or what?" he asked.

I stepped backward toward the gray, keeping my .44 centered on the man and the woman called Ramona. "I figured to," I said, and shot the animal between its eyes.

Behind the two, I saw Hoodoo descend the slope and walk toward us, Sharps rifle held at the ready. "Can I put my damn hands down?" asked the woman.

"Not just yet, ma'am," I told her. "I'm afraid I'm going to have to search you first."

She snorted. "That might not be so bad," she said. "You're a good lookin' boy."

Hoodoo limped toward us. "I'll search her, Merlin," he said, "I'm familiar with the territory."

The woman turned. "Hoodoo Hawks!" she said. "I ain't seen you since Miles City! What are you doin' ridin' with a posse?"

Hoodoo poked her with the Sharps. "Ain't no posse," he said. "There's just the deputy and me. Get your clothes off, Ramona."

She grinned, removing her riding coat. "You used to ask nicer," she said. Hoodoo set his rifle down and began to search the woman. "You used to *be* nicer," he replied. "I hear you gut-shot that bank teller at Silver City."

The woman shrugged. "A lady has to make a livin'," she said.

All at once, it dawned on me. "You're the *Coldwaters!*"

"Yeah," said the big man, "I'm Vince Coldwater. You boys just killed my brother Clete."

Vince spat. "If it wasn't for bad luck I'd have no luck at all," he said, "I sure never expected to be took down by a kid and a burned-out drunk."

Quickly, Hoodoo checked the wounded outlaw for concealed weapons while I kept him and Ramona covered. "How'd you come to find us, anyway?" Vince asked.

"Long story," Hoodoo said. "We was lookin' for somebody else."

Once I had patched up Vince Coldwater's belly wound, I fished two sets of manacles out of my saddlebags and locked both Vince's and Ramona's hands behind them. Inside the cabin, I found the Coldwaters' saddlebags, each filled with greenbacks from the Silver City bank. Just for the record, I asked Vince if he'd had anything to do with Julie's kidnapping, but of course he hadn't. Hoodoo had been right. Whoever had taken Julie McAllister had merely pretended to be the Coldwaters. I was no closer to knowing who her kidnappers were than before.

By ten o'clock we were riding out of the canyon, bound for Fort Savage. I was riding Clete Coldwater's horse, with Clete's body draped behind me, and we were bringing two prisoners.

I suppose I should have been happy, but I wasn't. There I was, my first time out as a deputy U. S. marshal, and I had led a posse of two in the killing of one notorious outlaw and the capture of the other. We had recovered most, if not all, of the stolen money from the bank at Silver City, and I had come through a bad shooting affray unharmed.

What I had *not* done was the one thing I'd set out to do. I had not recovered Julie McAllister. Worse, I had found her and lost her again. Worse still, I had no idea where she was, or where to even begin looking for her. Seems like even when life lets a man succeed, it may not give him the success he wants, nor in the way he wants it.

I was worried about Hoodoo. He had played a large part in the raid, but he could no longer get on and off his horse without help, and his face was ashen and drawn. By the time we rode the three miles back to Bear-that-sings's camp he could barely stay on his horse. When we reined up in front of the old Indian's lodge, I wasn't quick enough. The reins slipped through Hoodoo's fingers, and he fell out of the saddle and onto the earth before I could reach him.

Bear-that-sings had been waiting for us. His furrowed face had shown a fierce pride as we approached. I suppose he recalled his own younger days of successful raids, counting coup, and such. Anyway, no sooner had Hoodoo hit the ground than Bear-that-sings was at my side, helping to lift him up. Together, we carried him to the lodge and laid him down just inside.

Hoodoo felt hot as a furnace. He opened his eyes

and looked into mine. "It's blood poisoning," he said. "I didn't want to tell you. Knew you'd turn back, try to take care of me.

"Go on without me, kid. Bear-that-sings and me go back a ways. I druther trust him to heal me than any white sawbones I know."

"You should have told me—" I began.

He smiled a crooked smile. "Hell, kid, I just did. Now don't you go to worrying about me. I'll be up soon, better than before. Then you and me can go hunt for that Julie gal again."

We both knew that wouldn't happen. Julie's trail had gone cold, her whereabouts a mystery. The search for Julie McAllister had come to an end.

"I'll hold you to that," I said. My voice sounded strained, even to my ears. "If I don't hear from you in a week or two, I'll find you and shoot you in your other leg."

Hoodoo closed his eyes. "I ain't worried," he said. "I've seen you shoot."

As luck would have it, the same young sentry as before was on duty at Fort Savage when I rode in with the Coldwaters. I had done what I could for Vince, but he had been shot in the belly, after all. The man was tougher than a boiled owl, but I could see he was not doing all that well.

"Halt! Who goes there?" said the sentry.

"Deputy Marshal Fanshaw," I said. "How are you doing, soldier?"

The sentry recognized me. When he did, he dropped all his military decorum.

"Well, howdy, Deputy!" he said, lowering his rifle. "You bringin' another dead man for us to take keer of? We buried the last one."

"That's good," I said. "That's the best thing to do with a dead man."

The boy didn't wait for me to ask this time, but called the corporal of the guard straight away. "Corporal of the Guard!" he said. "Deputy Marshal Fanshaw, with prisoners! To see the major!"

"And the post surgeon," I said. "One of my prisoners has a bullet wound."

The sentry grinned. "Where's your partner?" he asked. "Business at the hog ranch hasn't been the same since he left."

I tried to keep it light. "He decided to stay on the reservation awhile," I said. "He ran into an old friend."

All at once, the strain of the day set in. I felt drained and bone weary. I had left the bay and Hoodoo's paint with him at Bear-that-sings's camp and was riding Rutherford. Ramona and Vince rode their own horses, their wrists shackled to their saddles. Clete's body lay face down, draped across his horse. When I stepped down off Rutherford, my legs didn't want to hold me. I took hold of the saddle horn and leaned against the little horse until I could stand erect. Then I turned to my prisoners and unlocked their handcuffs.

The post surgeon seemed to appear out of nowhere. He was a portly man in his mid-forties, dressed in a white coat and straw hat. Two troopers—medical orderlies, I reckoned—followed him, carrying a stretcher.

Vince Coldwater pressed his hand to his wounded belly. He nodded curtly at the litter bearers. "If that damn stretcher is for me," he said, "you can take it back. Ain't nobody carryin' *me* nowhere."

I was about to tell him to behave himself and let the boys tote him when it turned out to be unnecessary. As the outlaw stepped down off his horse, his knees buckled and he folded into the dust like a dropped blanket. The orderlies scooped him up, laid him on the stretcher, and hurried him off to the infirmary as if they'd done it a hundred times.

Ramona seemed unconcerned. "Vince tends to pass out when he gets real mad," she said. "I expect he's mad because you caught us."

"Seems he might have expected to be arrested sometime," I told her.

"Oh, he did," Ramona said, "but it made him mad anyway."

The corporal of the guard then arrived with a detail and took Ramona into custody. Last I saw of her, a dozen or so bemused troopers watched as the detail escorted her to the guardhouse. I expect they didn't have female guests at the guardhouse all that often.

I found that a good many soldiers had turned out and were watching me, as well. Those boys looked at

195

me as if I had fetched home the Holy Grail or something, instead of just a few shopworn outlaws. Still, I can't say I didn't enjoy their attentions.

I was thinking about how much I would like a little peace and quiet and maybe a long rest when I looked across the parade ground and saw I wasn't likely to get either one. Major Burdette came striding toward me, and at his side was the gent who had sent me off on my girl hunt in the first place—my boss, U.S. Marshal Chance Ridgeway.

fourteen

Ridgeway looked just the same as when I saw him last, and for some reason that surprised me. So much had happened since I rode out of Dry Creek it seemed I had been gone for months instead of merely days. "Howdy, Marshal," I said, "you're looking well."

Ridgeway smiled. "Thank you, son," he replied. "I wish I could say the same about you. You look like forty miles of bad road."

The marshal glanced about, then fixed his faded blue eyes on me again. "Where's Hoodoo?" he asked.

"Left him back in the badlands with an old friend of his—Crow medicine man name of Bear-that-sings. Hoodoo's got blood-poisoning, but he has a lot of faith in his doctor."

Ridgeway nodded. Turning to Major Burdette, he

asked, "You have a place where I can talk to my deputy? I need to hear his report."

"Certainly," said Burdette. "Use my office."

The sergeant who served as company clerk and acted as telegrapher stood at the major's side. Burdette turned to him. "Marshal Ridgeway and Deputy Fanshaw will be meeting for a time in my office," he said. "They are not to be disturbed."

"Yes, sir," the sergeant said.

"Have the mess sergeant dish up two plates and deliver them to my office," he said. "Tell him two cups and a pot of coffee, as well."

The sergeant saluted and turned sharply away toward the mess hall. I caught Major Burdette's eye and grinned my appreciation. I had not thought about food until the major brought up the subject. Now that he had, I felt hungry enough to eat a moose.

While Ridgeway looked on, I washed up in the waters of Sidewinder Creek, removing at least some of the trail dust I'd acquired. Then we walked together across the parade ground to Major Burdette's office and went inside. The office was just as I remembered it—same fly-specked calendar, same photographs of Presidents Lincoln, Grant, and Arthur. The Sibley stove still hunkered in its sandbox, cold now in the heat of late summer. I sat down in the same chair I'd occupied when I first met Major Burdette. Ridgeway sat down across from me, behind the major's desk.

The feeling I'd had earlier came on me again. It

seemed a long time ago that I had sat there talking to the major, yet it had been only a matter of days. Ridgeway leaned his bony elbows on the desk and watched me. He seemed to be in no particular hurry. I tried to gather my thoughts in order to make a proper report, but I knew that no matter how I told the story it would end the same way. I had failed, and I knew it.

Yes, we had brought in the Coldwaters. We had recovered some, maybe most, of the stolen money from the Silver City bank. All that was to the good, but I had failed at the job I'd been sent to do. We had met Julie's kidnappers not once but twice. Each time I had been a day late and a dollar short. Then, through blind good luck, we had rescued Julie. A day later, I had lost her again. Now she, her kidnappers, and the ransom money were gone, and only God knew where.

A red-haired private, his face a riot of freckles, appeared in the doorway, a covered tray in his hands. He looked at Ridgeway. "Major Burdette's compliments," he said, setting the tray down upon the desk. "Salt pork, potatoes and gravy, with apple dumplin's. There's coffee in the pot."

"Thank you, son," said Ridgeway. "Tell the major we're much obliged."

The private saluted. We weren't military, so the gesture wasn't needful, but apparently the private wasn't taking any chances. He walked quickly away, back toward the mess hall. Ridgeway uncovered the plates, studied their contents, and nodded. "Last time you and me broke bread together, we were eating horse meat at Hoodoo's place," he said. "This army grub is more to my liking."

We ate in silence, my thoughts on my report. I reckon it's only natural for a man to want to put the best light on his actions, and at first I tried to find words that would do just that. But try as I might I had never been able to shade the facts with Ridgeway. In the end, I simply told him the plain, unvarnished truth. I recounted everything that happened from the day Hoodoo and me left Dry Creek.

I told him about meeting the outlaws at Alkali Creek and how my temper caused me to get knocked unconscious by a rifle butt. I told him about Hoodoo reading the outlaws' boot prints and saying they did not belong to Vince and Clete Coldwater. I told of our ride to Fort Savage and on to Keppler's horse ranch, where I bought fresh horses. I told him of how we had rescued Julie, of Hoodoo's wounding, and of losing Julie again.

I told him about the killing of Rafael and of meeting Major Burdette on our way to the fort. I said Burdette had reported that one of his patrols had caught sight of two men and a woman riding into the badlands, and I told him of our decision to pursue them.

I spoke of meeting Bear-that-sings and of his telling Hoodoo where the three were holed up. I described our early morning raid, of losing the gray horse, of my shooting Vince Coldwater, and of Hoodoo's killing Vince's brother Cletus. I told him I had arrested the survivors and had fetched them back to Fort Savage. As for Hoodoo, I said he had decided to stay with the old medicine man and try for a healing of his infected wound.

The trouble with telling the whole truth and nothing but the truth is that by the time you finish doing so your coffee has gone cold. It would have been easier by far to fancy up the facts a bit, leaving out all them parts that made me look like a dern fool, and the report would not have taken nearly so long, either.

I took a sip of my cold army coffee and waited. I expected Ridgeway to criticize me. I figured I had it coming. Truth is, I wished he would. The marshal took out his old briar and filled it from his tobacco pouch. I waited while he put the pouch away and tamped the bowl to his satisfaction. I watched him strike a match on the sole of his boot. By the time he had gone through all the pipe smoker's foofaraw and fumadiddle and finally had the briar going well my nerves were stretched tighter than fence wire.

Ridgeway never did what I expected. He looked at me through the blue smoke and said, "Good report, deputy. I'll need that in writing, at your earliest convenience."

" 'Good report?' " I said. "Is that all you have to say? Don't you even have any questions?"

"No. Seems to me you did well. You exercised initiative and diligence. You were intrepid and brave. You moved boldly, but you exercised proper caution, for the most part. I could ask no more of any man."

"Well, if *I* was in your boots I believe I'd ask a whole *lot* more. How about the fact that I had Julie McAllister in my care and lost her again? How about my failure to capture the kidnappers and recover the ransom money?"

Ridgeway looked unruffled. "In the first instance, you left Julie briefly to recover her book. You could have had no way of knowing she would disappear again. In the second, you and Hoodoo opened fire on the outlaws and drove them off. You might well have killed or captured them if Hoodoo hadn't been wounded."

"And the dog *might* have caught the rabbit if he hadn't stopped to pee on a bramble," I said. "It seems to me I made some serious mistakes, Marshal!"

"A man can only really know his mistakes after the fact," Ridgeway said. "You made choices. You made the best choices you could, based on the knowledge you had at the time.

"Look at what you accomplished, son! You did what lawmen from here to Oklahoma have wanted to do—you put the Coldwater boys out of business! You recovered the money stolen from the Silver City bank! You helped to end horse theft in this part of the country! As for Julie—well, she's gone. The trail has gone cold. I know that's a disappointment to you, but there ain't a whole lot we can do about it right now.

"I want you to go on back to Dry Creek. Spend the night here at the fort and head back in the morning.

Take some time off. I'll get hold of you through Glenn at the city marshal's office."

"But what about Thane McAllister?" I asked. "I doubt if he'll be so generous in his judgments. What will he think?"

"Let me worry about Thane. He ain't your concern."

I stood up. I walked over to the open door. Out on the parade ground, troopers were drilling on horseback. I watched them wheel and turn their mounts in formation and wished my thoughts were as well-ordered. I turned back to Ridgeway. "I thought you'd fire me for sure." I said. "I figure I have it coming."

"Go on, son. I'll see you back in Dry Creek."

"What about the prisoners?"

"Major Burdette will hold them here until Vince is well enough to travel. Then he'll deliver them to Silver City for trial."

"Well, all right. Maybe I'll ride over to Bear-that-sings's camp in the morning. See how Hoodoo is doing."

"Good idea. Take care, son."

The cavalry has more bugle calls than a dog has fleas. I bunked with the troopers in the barracks that evening, and I believe there was some kind of bugle call every two hours until lights out at 9:30. Then at 5:45 in the morning they played "Assembly for Trumpeters," followed by "Reveille" at 6:00. They played "Mess Call" at 6:30, and I went over and had coffee and cornbread with the soldiers. I suppose they had a bugle call for Going to the Latrine, too, but I don't believe I heard that one.

The young corporal helped me pack Hoodoo's and my camp outfit and bedroll on the packhorse, after which I stopped briefly at the sutler's store. Once there, I bought a supply of salt pork, tinned peaches, and brown sugar from the post trader and after a fairly extended period of haggling, picked up a good wool blanket as well. The trader rarely saw a customer with much ready cash, and his eagerness to bargain gave me a certain edge in our negotiations. He was still trying to interest me in more of his merchandise when I set out from the fort, bound for Bear-that-sings's camp. The weather was already hot, as befits summer in the badlands, and I rode into the burning land along the game trail we had followed earlier.

The horses saw me first. I rode Rutherford out atop the low hill that overlooked the valley and saw Bear-that-sings's tepee, gray white against the dark brush of the bottom land. The horses—Bear-that-sings's pintos and his sorrel, and Hoodoo's paint and the bay gelding—grazed beside the slow-moving stream. Seeing me top out above them on Rutherford, the horses whinnied a greeting. Sociable as ever, Rutherford answered their call. I turned the buckskin downhill and headed him toward the lodge.

At first I could see no one. Then, as I drew nearer, I

saw a sight that caused me to catch my breath. Hoodoo lay on his back, eyes closed and his face to the sky in the dry grass behind the lodge. He lay still as death, his hands crossed atop his chest, and Bear-that-sings and his missus were living up to the family name. Their voices rose in a quavery lament that sent shivers up and down my spine and chilled me to the bone!

I knew the worst form of blood poisoning was deadly, and that folks who had it generally died within a few days to a week. Even so, I couldn't believe the sickness could have taken Hoodoo so soon! Why hadn't I insisted he get to a doctor sooner? I should have forced him to see the surgeon at Fort Savage, at gunpoint if necessary! Now Hoodoo was gone, and it was all my fault!

I was off Rutherford and running as fast as I could toward the sorrowful scene. Bear-that-sings and his missus stopped their singing, staring at me as I came toward them. Then, just as I reached them, the "corpse" came to life! Hoodoo suddenly sat bolt upright, and a wicked grin lit up his whiskered face!

He bounded up onto his feet and commenced to do a kind of mad dance there behind the tepee! I glanced at Bear-that-sings and his wife and saw that they were watching me, a broad smile on each face, and I knew I'd been bamboozled. Missus Bear covered her mouth in a dainty, female manner and giggled. Mister Bear slapped his bony thigh and laughed like a fool. And Hoodoo jumped up and kicked his heels together in a kind of loony glee.

"Well, howdy there, Deputy!" Hoodoo said. "I heard you comin' for two miles and smelled you for three! As you kin see, I'm doin' fine!"

"Your leg seems better," I said, "but I ain't so sure about your mental state. You like to scared me to death!"

"When I seen you comin' I decided to josh you a mite. I got Bear-that-sings and his woman to help me. Worried, were you?"

I grinned. "Worried I'd have to pack your fool body out, like we did Rafael's. Would have been just like you to cause me extra work."

Hoodoo crossed his legs and sat down Indian style. He did look better. He seemed to move more freely, and his color was good. I found that I really was glad to see him.

"How did Bear-that-sings heal you?" I asked.

"Mashed up some roots and smeared 'em on the wound. Made me drink some vile potion. Tickled me with a feather while he chanted songs. Throwed dust in the air. Fact is, I am cured. The poison is gone, and my leg is healin' nicely, as you can see."

I hunkered down in the grass across from him. "First time I ever saw you move that way," I said. "Put me in mind of a dancin' bear I saw once."

Hoodoo was silent for a moment. Then he asked, "Did you get the Coldwaters to the fort all right?"

"Yes. Ridgeway was there. Said we'd done a good job."

"You look troubled. What else did he say?"

205

"I asked him about finding Julie. He said the trail's gone cold. Said there's not much we can do."

The tracker studied me. "I know you don't want to quit. But Ridgeway's right. Unless we get some word of her whereabouts—"

"I know. It's just that I made a promise to myself. After all we've been through, letting her go doesn't set well."

I stood. Walking back to where Rutherford stood ground-tied, I took the bundle from my saddle. "Brought your doctor some groceries," I said, "salt pork, peaches, and brown sugar. All that and a blanket, too."

"He'll be pleased," Hoodoo said. "You goin' back to Dry Creek?"

"For now. What about you? Heading back to your place?"

"In a day or two. Thought maybe I'd do some huntin' with Bear-that-sings first. This camp could use some meat."

"Ridgeway said he'd leave your pay at the fort. Said there might be reward money for the Coldwaters later, too. I'll take the bay gelding back with me as far as the fort. The horse belongs to Uncle Sam now."

Hoodoo walked with me as I led Rutherford and the packhorse across the creek to where the other horses grazed. I put a halter on the bay, took the lead rope in hand, and turned to swing up into the saddle. "Well," I said. "Watch your topknot, like the mountain men say."

We shook hands. "You'll do, Deputy," Hoodoo said. Leading the bay, I set out for Dry Creek. I didn't look back.

Dry Creek hadn't changed much since I'd been gone. I don't know why I thought it might have; the dern town never *had* changed much. The schoolhouse had needed painting when I left. It needed painting even more now that I'd come back. There had been three saddlehorses tied in front of the Oasis Saloon when I rode out. There were three horses at the rail when I came back. Leading the bay I'd bought from Keppler, I reined up in front of Walt's livery barn. Walt had been dead for over a year, and the widow Blair now owned the business, but the sign out front still said Walt's Livery. In Dry Creek, getting your name painted on a building was about as close to immortality as a man could come.

It was just past sundown when I rode in, and the sky still held some of its brightness. Along the street, shadows deepened. The smell of hot wood and dust lingered as the sunbaked street began to cool. Old Bummer, night man at the livery, had just lit the coal oil lantern and hung it inside the big, open doors. He looked up and recognized me as I stepped down off Rutherford. "Evenin', Merlin," he said. He hadn't even knowed I'd been gone.

I unpacked the packhorse, turned Rutherford and the bay over to his care, and walked two blocks to the widow Blair's house. She was setting out on her porch in the twilight, shelling peas, and she greeted me when she saw me stop at her gate. "Hello, Merlin," she said. "Nice evenin', ain't it?"

"Yes, ma'am," I said, touching my hat brim. She hadn't knowed I'd been gone, either. "Miz Blair," I said. "I was wondering if I could maybe roll out my bed at the livery barn, like before. Just for a few days."

"Why, yes," she said. "Any time, Merlin. You looking for work?"

"No, ma'am. I have a deputy marshal's job with Marshal Ridgeway. He's out of town right now, but I expect I'll be sent somewheres when he gets back. I just need a place to sleep 'til then."

The widow stood, brushing a strand of snow-white hair from her eyes. She balanced the pan that held the peas on her hip, her hand on the screen door. "Nice seeing you, Merlin," she said.

"Nice seeing you, ma'am," I said. "Good evening."

By the time I got to the Oasis, the hitchrack was empty and so was the barroom. Boogles McFee greeted me as I came in and offered me a beer on the house. As I may have said before, Boogles was something of a cheapskate.

Two years previous, at Christmas time, he'd sampled a few too many of his own eggnogs and had offered a free round to everybody in his saloon. When he sobered up and realized what he'd done, he was so stricken by remorse he could hardly function for a day or so.

208

But Boogles was a grateful man, and he never forgot a favor. He remembered it was me who had gone after his swamper Delbert Snodgrass back in June. I had fetched the thief and Boogles's money back, and I reckon he figured that was worth a nickel beer. I drank my beer, bought a second one, and drank it, too. Then I bade Boogles goodnight and walked out onto the street.

The evening was dark, and soft as rabbit fur when I left the Oasis. Old man Fogarty was out lighting the oil lamps along Main Street, and here and there around town yellow light glowed in the windows. A cool breeze swept down from the mountains, promising relief after the day's heat. Scattered stars had begun to gather in the night sky. I thought about having a bite to eat down at Ignacio's Cafe, but decided against it. Just wasn't hungry, I guess.

I turned and sauntered up the street to the livery, spread my blankets in the loft, and turned in. As usual, the last thing I thought of before falling asleep was Julie McAllister.

fifteen

The week after I got back to Dry Creek the one man I *didn't* want to see came to see me. I was out back of the livery barn, putting a set of shoes on the bay horse, and the sun on my back was hot as the hinges of Hell. I had set the last nail and was just about to put my tools away when something blocked the light behind me. I turned, and found I was standing in the ample shade of Thane McAllister.

"Fanshaw," said he. "I'd like a word with you."

The moment I feared had come. *Let me worry about Thane,* Ridgeway had said. *He ain't your concern.* Easy for him to say. I was the man who had rescued Thane's daughter, only to lose her again. What's more, I already felt more guilt than anyone else could ever cause me to feel. I could not look the big cattleman in the eye, but I tried to make my voice sound casual. "Sure, Thane," I said.

He must have read something in my face. "I ain't here to lay blame, Deputy," he said. "I reckon you done your best. I'm just here as Julie's father."

He hesitated. "You were the last to see her," he said. "How—how did she seem to you?"

"She seemed fine," I said. "In good spirits. And in good health."

Thane sighed. When he spoke, his voice was so soft I could hardly make out the words. They were either "That's good" or "Thank God."

"One more question. The men who took her. Did they—"

"Julie said the men never mistreated her."

Relief showed in every inch of the man. "I'm obliged to you, Deputy," he said. "Much obliged." He turned, walking away.

"Thane," I said. The big man stopped, turned.

"She also said she loves you."

He made no answer, but nodded. Then he walked into the darkness of the livery barn and was gone.

Over the next few weeks I mostly spent my days at the city marshal's office, playing cribbage with Glenn Murdoch and losing, as usual. Dry Creek never was what a person would call a high crime area, so there wasn't much lawbreaking to deal with. I mostly helped Glenn make his rounds at night, and sometimes we had a drunk to lock up for the night and clean up after. Glenn liked to keep a clean jail. Naturally, it was usually me who got to use the broom and mop.

We did get called out one night to deal with a domestic disturbance. Homer Hess and his missus had been married forty-two years at that point, and Glenn swore they had fought every day of that time. If that was the literal truth, I calculated they had fought each other fifteen thousand three hundred and thirty times over the forty-two years and as a result should both pretty well be experts in the art of marital warfare.

According to Missus Hess, Homer had got violent again. He was still recovering from when she had broke his leg with a sledge hammer, and she claimed he had struck at her with his crutch. When the neighbors sent for the law she had been screaming that Homer was trying to kill her.

When we got to their house, we separated the combatants, as it were, and Glenn was going to lock

Homer up at the jail overnight so the neighbors could get some sleep. At that point, Missus Hess commenced to cry and wail, pleading with us not to arrest her sweet Homer, so in the end we didn't. That was about the biggest crime Dry Creek had to deal with that fall.

For awhile there I received a good deal of local notice for my part in the arrest and capture of the Coldwater gang but fame is fleeting, as they say. It wasn't long before people around Dry Creek moved on to new sensations and scandals, but at least I'd had my day in the sun.

Ridgeway stopped by the office to tell me the trial of Vince Coldwater and the lovely Ramona had been postponed until Vince recovered from the bullet wound I had gave him. The marshal said I would be called as a witness when the trial began. Until then, he said, I was to stay in Dry Creek and lend Glenn a hand until further notice. He gave me my pay for the month, sixty dollars, and for a day or two I wallowed in my new-found prosperity, although I didn't spend much of the money. Ridgeway said nothing more about Julie McAllister, and I didn't mention my conversation with Thane.

About a week later, I was sitting around the office reading Glenn's law books and wishing I knew how to stack a cribbage deck when Glenn came in with the mail. Most of it wasn't all that exciting. There were the usual lost, strayed, or stolen livestock notices, a couple of wanted posters, and a circular from a patent medicine salesman selling liver pills. There was one letter, however. It came from the city marshal down in Lander, Wyoming Territory, and as things turned out it was a letter that changed everything.

Glenn sneaked his spectacles out of his shirt pocket like a gambler palming an ace, and put them on. He always seemed embarrassed to have anyone see him wearing glasses, like he'd been caught naked, or without his hat. Glenn cleared his throat and said what he always said, "I only need these damn things to read."

He tore open the envelope, took the letter out, and unfolded the paper. Holding the letter almost at arm's length, he read in silence, his lips moving slightly. The missive was a short one. When he had finished, Glenn placed it on his desk and smoothed it with his fingers. He took off his spectacles and returned them to his pocket. Looking out the window in the general direction of Wyoming, he said quietly, "Well, I'll be go to Hell."

"Well?" said I. "Are you going to tell me what the letter says, or is it some kind of a dern secret?"

Glenn shook his head, coming out of his trance. "Do you remember Delbert Snodgrass? The kid who robbed Boogles's till and rode off in the gumbo last June?"

"Well, of course I do," I said, "It was me who rode out on your pet mule and brought him back."

"That's right," Glenn said. "Well, according to this letter from Marshal Biggs, down in Lander, Delbert traded a slow draw for a tombstone last week. Pulled his gun on a hardcase name of Bellcourt and got his lamp blowed out. Apparently, Delbert told people he used to work here in Dry Creek. Marshal Biggs wrote me to see if Delbert had kinfolk hereabouts."

"Poor Delbert," I said. "He always hankered to be a desperado. Now he's went and died like one."

"What about kinfolk? I never heard him speak of having family around here."

"No. He hinted once that he'd run away from home as a kid, but he never said where home was. Back east somewhere, I gathered."

Glenn stood up. "That's what I'll tell Biggs," he said. "I hate writing letters. I believe I'll go over to the telegraph office and send him my answer by wire."

"Go ahead. I'll hold down the office."

I stood at the window and watched Glenn walk away down the street. My thoughts went back to the previous June, when Glenn had sent me out to fetch Delbert back. I had found him afoot and rain-soaked, played out from trying to move in the thick gumbo mud. I had felt sorry for him then, and I was sorry now to hear of his death. Poor Delbert had been one of those hard luck people who not only never catch the brass ring, they never even get on the merry-go-round.

I recalled our walk in the rain that day, and the

things we talked about. Poor Delbert seemed drawn to the outlaw life and to what he thought was its glamor. Somehow, down there in Lander, he had got into a shooting scrape and cashed in his chips. It made me sad, just thinking about his short and empty life.

Thinking about Delbert led me to recall other things. It was like when you push a boulder off a hilltop. The boulder knocks a few other rocks loose, and they bump a few more, until all of a sudden there's a whole dern avalanche a-rolling downhill. Memories returned, unsorted and random. Remembered bits of conversation came to mind. Incidents I had nearly forgotten came back, demanding my attention. Faster and faster the memories came, linking up, forming a pattern.

I knew what I had to do. I found a pencil stub in Glenn's desk and wrote him a message. I said I was leaving town for a day or two and didn't know when I'd be back. At the livery barn, I picked up my saddle, packed a few possibles in a traveling bag, and took my money from my bedroll. At 3:42 that afternoon, I was on the southbound stage, headed for Wyoming Territory.

The coach pulled into Lander three days later, just at sundown. Even at that hour the town was busy as a beehive. There were two small hotels and one big one, the Fremont. I splurged and took a room at the latter for a dollar and a quarter per day. Leaving my traveling bag in my room, I walked out to see the sights.

The evening was cool, with a hint of frost in the air. To the west of town, the mighty peaks of the Wind River range stood dark against the day's last light. Off to the north lay the Wind River Indian Reservation, and beyond, at its northern edge, the Owl Creek Mountains, cold and remote in the distance.

I used the dying light to take a tour of the town. I counted ten saloons, two banks, a drug store, a clothing store, three grocery stores, and a brewery.

Cowpunchers and ranchmen rode the streets a-horseback, while townsfolk strolled the boardwalks or drove to and fro in buggies and wagons. Music drifted out onto the street from some of the saloons, and lamps lit up the windows of homes and stores.

I found the city marshal's office down the street, near the stage station, and went inside. A heavy-set man with curly red hair sat at a cluttered desk, writing in a ledger. He turned toward the door when he heard me come in. "Can I help you, cowboy?"

I smiled. "You can if you're Marshal Biggs." I said. "I'm Merlin Fanshaw, deputy U.S. marshal, out of Dry Creek, Montana."

"Well," the man said, "I am Marshal Biggs, all right. Welcome to Lander."

Biggs's swivel chair squealed like a rusty gate as he swung around and stood up. He offered his hand. "Dry Creek, you say? I had me a telegram from Dry

216

Creek this week, from City Marshal Glenn Murdoch. You acquainted with the marshal?"

I shook his hand. "Yes, I am. He's a good man, but he plays cribbage with neither mercy nor pity."

Biggs laughed. "Pinochle is my weakness," he said. "Don't let anyone tell you it's just a game."

Biggs dumped a double armful of papers off a Windsor chair and bade me set down on it. When I had done so, he said, "Murdoch says as far as he knows, Delbert Snodgrass has no kinfolk in Montana."

"That's right," I said. "Delbert came to Dry Creek a year ago from someplace back east. He worked for awhile as swamper in a Dry Creek saloon."

Biggs stood, took a chipped enamel cup from a shelf, and nodded at the coffee pot atop the office stove. "Coffee?" he asked. "Obliged," I said. Biggs poured the cup full and set it before me. He leaned his elbows on the desktop and studied me awhile.

"So what brings you to Lander?" he asked.

I took a sip of the coffee. It was black, hot, and so strong it could have woke Delbert. "Just followin' up on some old case work," I told him. "But back to the late Delbert. How was it he came to *be* the late Delbert?"

Marshal Biggs studied me again for a time, maybe wondering why I asked. Then he shrugged. "He worked for a time this summer at a horse ranch south of here, down on the Little Popo Agie. Rancher laid him off, and Delbert came to town. Took a job as swamper at the Gold Dollar Saloon."

Biggs took a Bull Durham sack out of his vest pocket and offered it to me. I shook my head "no," and he commenced to roll himself a smoke. "Accordin' to the barkeep, Delbert came to think he was some kind of gunfighter. He took to carrying an old cap and ball Starr revolver on his hip. Cut notches in the grips and claimed he had killed some fellers up Montana way.

"The saloon crowd laughed at him behind his back. To his face, they pretended to believe his brag. Treated him like he was John Wesley Hardin or somebody. Used to say, 'Oh, Mister Snodgrass, can I look at your revolver?' and 'Oh, my! Look at the notches on the handle! How many men have you killed, Mister Snodgrass?' Foolishness, of course, but then it don't take much to entertain drunks."

"Yes," I said. "Seems like Delbert had a real need to be somebody."

Biggs twisted the paper on his quirly, put it in his mouth, and lit it. "Not to speak ill of the dead, but the boy was maybe ten cards short of a deck. He would have done better to choose a different kind of some-body to be."

The marshal blew out a thin stream of blue smoke. "Last week a gunslick name of Bellcourt was in the Gold Dollar. Delbert took a notion to call him out. The bar crowd laughed up their sleeves, but Bellcourt had no sense of humor when it came to men with guns calling him out. A half-second later, Delbert Snodgrass was dead as a beaver hat.

"I couldn't even arrest Bellcourt. He had no way of knowing he was dealing with the feebleminded. I sent him on his way and advised him not to come back to Lander. Sad story, but that's how Delbert came to get himself planted out at the bone orchard."

I finished my coffee and stood up. "I'm obliged, Marshal," I said. "I'll be in the area for a day or two. I'll try to stop by again before I leave."

"Do that," said Biggs.

I had just opened the door and was about to step out onto the street. Marshal Biggs still sat at his desk. I turned and said, "Oh, by the way. That horse rancher you mentioned—the one down on the Little Popo. Do you recall his name?"

"Yeah. Name's Christmas. Bill Christmas."

"Yes," I said. "That's what I thought it would be."

The sorrel I rented in Lander was no Rutherford, but he was honest and clear footed, for a livery stable horse. When I put my saddle on him I figured him for a saddlehorse who had knowed better days, probably on a cow outfit. He had a tendency to dog it, easing back out of the gait a rider put him in, but when I drew rein a mile out of town and put my spurs on he seen the jig was up and fell to behaving himself.

The livery man had told me how to find the Christmas horse ranch. He said it lay south of town below Atlantic Peak at the end of the Wind River range. He said the Little Popo Agie river ran along the ranch's southeast side, and that the ranch house itself was set in the foothills of the mountains.

The morning had dawned cold and overcast, the sky gray as lead. There was a bite to the wind that made me wish I had brought my winter clothes. The land was pretty and open, good country for horses, but I reckon I had too much on my mind right then to appreciate it.

At about nine snow began to fall, scattered flakes carried on a rising wind at first, then thick and heavy as the storm increased. I wore only a light jacket and no gloves, and I felt the bite of the cold on my face and fingers as the temperature dropped. For a time I tried alternating the hand that held the reins. First, I guided the gelding with my left hand, keeping my right in my pocket. Then, when the fingers began to lose their feeling, I switched to my right hand, warming my left.

I took my scarf from around my throat and tied it under my chin, covering my ears, but the cold seemed to grow more intense by the minute. Vapor from my breathing puffed out and blew away in the storm. Sharp, bitter pain afflicted my nose, ears, and fingers. The snowfall, heavy now, made it hard to see. Sky, storm, and the ground below took on the same gray-white color. Even if I had been familiar with the country I would not have known where I was.

I cursed myself for a fool. I was no greenhorn. I had grown up on horseback, working outdoors in every kind of weather. My pa had taught me from when I was just a kid that the way to survive on the plains and in the mountains was to keep an eye on the weather and be ready for the unexpected. I had neglected that teaching, and I was paying the price.

Beneath the thin jacket I felt the cold reach for my vitals. I felt chilled to the bone. Snow frosted my eyelashes and threatened to close my eyes. My fingers, ears, and nose had lost their feeling and gone numb. Fear came and with it disbelief—how could taking a horseback ride on a day in early fall lead to such mortal danger?

I tried to form a plan. Maybe, I thought, I could take shelter somewhere, maybe build a fire and wait the storm out. I shook my head. Too many maybes. *Where* could I find shelter? The country was strange to me, mostly broken grassland and brushy draws, now filling fast with drifted snow. Build a fire? I carried no matches that day—and even if I'd had some, such wood as I might find would no doubt be too wet to burn. A low hill rose out of the storm ahead of me. Perhaps, I thought, if I ride to its crest I might be able to see a barn or a cabin somewhere in the distance. I touched the horse with my spurs, urging the animal up the slope, but the storm seemed to grow even more intense as I neared the hilltop. I could see nothing.

I turned the gelding downhill again. It stumbled, swayed, its movements choppy and nervous. The animal struggled to maintain its footing, sliding, tossing its head. I shifted my weight, trying to help the horse right itself. I hauled hard on the reins, jerking its head up. My efforts failed. The sorrel slued about, stumbled, and fell. I tried to kick free of the ice-packed stirrup, but felt my left foot slip through. Then I was falling with the horse, still trying to free my foot, as the ground rushed up to meet me.

My shoulders and head struck hard, snow exploding in an icy spray. I covered my face, tumbling with the sorrel in a world that had neither up nor down but only snow. Then the horse was on its feet again, my foot wedged tight in the stirrup. I prayed my boot would slip off and free me, but it did not. My numb fingers tried to draw my .44, but they had lost their feeling. I caught a glimpse of the sorrel's rear hooves pounding near my face, digging through the drifted snow. My body was bouncing, flying high with the sorrel's panicked running, then coming back to earth with a jolt.

Hidden rocks and sagebrush slashed at my face. I twisted, turned away. Then something struck the back of my head. Light, bright as summer lightning, exploded behind my eyes, and all the world went dark.

sixteen

Like a turtle in a pond, I seemed to rise from the cold and darkness at the bottom to the warmth and light of the surface. My head throbbed like a war drum behind my closed eyes, and my ears, nose, and fingers burned as if they had caught fire. I kept my breathing shallow and tried not to move. The pain had took charge of me, and I had no wish to provoke it.

Slowly, my memory returned. I recalled the storm, the horse falling, then rising again. I remembered the animal's panic and its running, my foot caught, my body dragging through the sage and drifted snow. Then there was the hard blow to my head, the blinding pain, and the blackness.

I knowed I was alive, at least. I hurt too much to be dead. *All right,* I said to myself, *if you're alive, where are you? Open your dern eyes and find out.*

I squinched my eyes open a crack. Light flooded my consciousness and stirred the pain up. I rode it out, closed my eyes again, then opened them once more.

I lay in a bed, inside a tidy, well-kept room. A well-favored Indian woman in her late forties or early fifties sat at my bedside, bathing my hand in a pan of warm water. She smiled as I stirred. Drying my hand, she stood.

Her eyes were on me, but her words were for someone outside the room.

"He's awake," she said.

A moment later, Julie McAllister entered the room. She wore a pinafore of blue-checked gingham, and she carried a steaming cup of coffee in a china mug. Her words were for the Indian woman, but her smile was for me. "Thank you, Mother Christmas," she said. "I'll take over now."

Julie handed me the coffee. Her smile was as warm as I remembered it. "Welcome back, cowboy," she said. "You do have a flair for dramatic entrances."

I couldn't help it. Just seeing her brought a measure of my spunk back. "I reckon," I said. "Sort of like your flair for disappearing. I brought your poetry book back. It's in my saddlebags, wherever they are now."

"Your horse and your saddle are out in the barn," she said. "Drink some of that coffee while I go tell Billy you're awake."

With a toss of her long hair Julie was gone, leaving the faint scent of her perfume behind her. Somewhere, a door opened and closed. I cradled the coffee in both hands, soaking up its warmth. A moment later, I heard the door open again. Booted feet stomped heavily, then strode quickly across the room. I took a long sip of the coffee and raised my eyes. My old partner from spring roundup at the M Cross, Billy Christmas, stood in the doorway, looking at me.

He was the same Billy Christmas, yet not quite the

same. He wore the same silver-belly Stetson he'd worn at the M Cross. His hair had the same blue-black sheen, and when he smiled his gray eyes smiled, too. He carried himself with his old confidence, and he moved with the careless grace of the bronc rider. But something about the face was different. There were changes—a scar here and there, the nose broken—but the change I noticed most was the peace, the happiness, that marked its expression. Billy moved a chair closer to the bed, swung it around, and sat down on it backward.

"Nice of you to come calling, Merlin," he said, "but you didn't have to bring that storm with you."

"I never meant to, Billy. You're looking good."

He grinned. "You look like Hell. I'm glad I found you when I did."

"How *did* you come to find me?"

"I had some mares and colts out on that big sagebrush flat. When the storm moved in I figured I'd best check on them. I spotted you just before your horse fell with you.

"By the time I got that sorrel stopped you'd lost your hat and most of your dignity, but you were still breathing. Gettin' hung up in a stirrup is a good way not to get any older."

"Glad you came along. My left leg feels half again as long as my right."

I sipped coffee from the mug, watching Billy. Behind him, Julie came in, caressed Billy's hair as she passed, and sat down on the bed.

Billy's face turned serious. "You here to arrest us?" he asked.

"I haven't decided yet."

Julie's dark eyes looked into mine. "You want to tell us what you know, or do you want to ask us some questions?"

I finished the coffee. I was by no means ready for a frolic or a footrace, but I did feel some better. I threw the blanket aside and sat up. "I'll tell you what I think I know," I said. "You tell me if I'm wrong.

"First off, there *was* no kidnapping. Billy helped you run away from your daddy, and the two of you made him pay twenty thousand dollars for your return," I said. "Except you never intended to return. You knew that Vince and Clete Coldwater were operating in the area, and you took advantage of the fact to pose as the Coldwaters and send those two ransom notes."

"The twenty thousand was my money," Julie said. "My mother left it to me when she died. Daddy refused to give it to me."

"Yes. I never meant to, but I happened to overhear your argument that day. Thane didn't approve of your wanting to marry Billy, to put it mildly."

Julie's dark eyes flashed. "I didn't *need* his approval! I had turned eighteen the month before! According to territorial law, a girl is a woman at eighteen—she's an adult, able to enter into contracts without her parent's approval, including marriage!"

"Speaking of the law," I said, "according to that same territorial law, you two committed extortion,

226

whether Thane owed you the twenty thousand or not. You caused your daddy considerable worry and distress, not to mention your godfather, Marshal Ridgeway."

"And you?" Julie asked.

"Yes," I said. "And me."

Julie lowered her eyes. There was pain and anger in her voice when she spoke. "We never intended to hurt anyone," she said, "but I can't say the same for Daddy. The day after the argument, he sent Billy off with Waco Calhoun and Red Murphy. Those two beat Billy half to death, on Daddy's orders."

"You could have gone to the law."

"In Progress County, Daddy pretty much *is* the law."

I turned to Billy. "How much of all this was your idea?"

He shrugged. "I never cared a damn about the money," he said, "but it was important to Julie. That made it important to me."

Billy stood. He walked to the window and looked out. "When I left Dry Creek, I came back here to the home place," he said. "I got over the whipping Red and Waco laid on me, but I couldn't get over Julie. She was the first thing on my mind when I woke up of a morning, and the last thing before I went to sleep. I had to go back for her."

Julie was looking at Billy as if she thought he'd hung the moon. "We met during one of my daily rides above the ranch," she said. "Vince and Cletus Coldwater had just robbed the Silver City bank. Everyone was talking about them. I decided we could get my money by pretending the Coldwaters had taken me for ransom. We asked for ten thousand at first, and got it. Then we asked for a second ten thousand to be delivered to Alkali Springs."

I nodded. "That's where I came in. Your daddy called in his old friend, U.S. Marshal Chance Ridgeway. The marshal deputized me, teamed me up with a tracker named Hoodoo Hawks, and sent us off to pay the 'kidnappers' and fetch you back."

I paused, remembering. "There was a third person," I said, "someone who posed as the other Coldwater brother. My guess is that someone was Delbert Snodgrass."

Billy looked surprised. "That's right," he said. "How did you know?"

"Delbert told me you offered him a job, should he ever get down this way," I said. "I guess I just put two and two together."

My boots stood beside the bed. I bent over and pulled them on. My head still hurt some, as did my left knee and ankle, but I felt better than I had a right to. I looked at Billy. "You clubbed me with a rifle butt at Alkali Springs," I said, "but I figure saving me from that runaway this morning cancels that out."

Billy frowned. "Nobody was supposed to get hurt," he said, "but you were fixing to jump me that day, rifle or no rifle. I'm sorry, Merlin."

"I need to limber up my leg some," I said. "What

about you and me taking a walk together outside? Will you excuse us, Julie?"

"Of course," she said. "You boys go ahead. I'll put supper on."

Billy handed me my hat. "The storm has passed," he said. "The sun's come out."

"Glad to hear it," I said.

We stepped out into the big room that served as kitchen and keeping room combined. The Indian woman sat with her sewing in a chair near the fireplace. Billy introduced me to her. "Mom," he said, "this is Merlin Fanshaw, a friend of mine from Montana. Merlin, meet my mother, Agnes." She gave me a shy smile as she offered her hand. I tipped my hat and said I was pleased to meet her, which I was. Then I followed Billy out the front door.

Billy was right. The storm had passed. Under the sun, the snow-covered prairie dazzled the eye with its brightness, and the proud mountains of the Wind River range stood shining in the distance. The ranch buildings were of log, solid and in good repair. I saw a barn with a hayloft, a blacksmith shop, a tool shed, and a small cabin near the main house. A buckboard and a light farm wagon were parked behind the barn. Near the barn stood a round corral for working broncs and a bigger, well-kept corral behind it. There were saddle and draft horses in the big corral. In a pasture beyond, a good-looking Belgian work team pawed through snow to get at the grass below.

"You have a fine place here, Billy," I said.

"Yes," he said. "I do."

"And a fine wife."

He nodded. "Julie and me were married in Lander the week we came back to Wyoming. How did you know?"

"Wedding band on Julie's left hand. I'm getting more observant since I turned lawman."

"I'll ask you again, Merlin. Are you here to arrest us?"

"No," I said, "but I do have another question. Was it you or Delbert who shot my tracker?"

Billy scowled. He looked out across the snow-covered landscape and sighed. "Delbert," he said. "He came to believe he really was some kind of desperado. When you boys surprised us at the spring, I told him to catch his horse and skedaddle, but Delbert wanted to shoot somebody."

"He got the job done. Put a bullet through Hoodoo's thigh."

"That wasn't supposed to happen. I fired Delbert on the spot, and we took separate trails back to Lander."

"Marshal Biggs said Delbert reckoned he was a gunfighter. Said he called out a hardcase named Bellcourt and came in a poor second."

"That's the straight of it."

We went into the barn. Billy had put the sorrel in a stall and gave it some oats. The little gelding looked none the worse for wear, but then it hadn't been drug across the flat by one foot, as I had. My saddle and bridle rested atop the stall partition. I reached into my saddlebag and took out Julie's poetry book, *Sonnets from the Portuguese.*

"That's the book Julie 'accidentally' dropped onto the ledge in the Pryors," I said. "I expect you two rode off as soon as I went down after it."

"Afraid so. While she was with you and Hoodoo, we used mirrors to keep in touch."

I shook my head. "You must have thought me one prize fool."

"We both admired your grit," Billy said. "You never gave up."

I grinned. "And I never caught on. Not until later, anyway."

It was then Julie called us in to supper. She stood in the doorway of the ranch house in her pinafore, smiled, and said, "Supper's ready, boys." The late sunlight caught her in its glow and held her in its warmth. For just a moment I wished that I was her husband and that Billy was only a friend who had come a-visiting. Then I printed the picture she made on my memory and tucked it away. I gave Billy a nudge and said, "We'd better go in. We don't want to upset the cook of this outfit."

It was a fine dinner. Julie and Mother Christmas served up a mess of chicken and dumplings that would have either fed a threshing crew or two hungry cowpunchers, which we was. There was biscuits, with chokecherry jelly and plum preserves, and some green beans Billy's mom had put up from their garden. The whole spread was topped off with a slab of apple pie and all the coffee a man could drink. I ain't sure if the way to a man's heart is through his belly, like the saying goes, but I do believe it's the way to mine. I pushed back away from the table and said my thank-yous. It had been quite a day.

"I expect I'd best get back to Lander before it gets dark," I said. "I'll be catching the stage to Dry Creek in the morning."

Billy stood up and went to the door. "I'll put your saddle on the sorrel," he said. "Stay a minute, and talk to Julie."

Mother Christmas got up and followed Billy outside. For the first time since that day in the Pryors, Julie and me were alone.

After a long moment, I said, "Well—it has been quite an adventure."

"Yes," Julie said, "it has that."

"Look here, Julie," I said. "It's none of my dern business, but I hope you can find some way to make peace with your daddy."

Julie's dark eyes grew cloudy. Her lips tightened in a stubborn line. "That's not likely," she said.

"You've got the life you wanted. Thane's lost his only daughter. Can't you cut him some slack?"

"After what Red and Waco did to Billy, at his orders—"

"Think about what *you* did to *him*. That old man *loves* you, Julie."

Julie looked away toward the window. Tears glistened in her dark eyes.

I touched her hand. "Why don't you write to him? Tell him you'd like to come back for a visit."

"I wouldn't do that without Billy," she said, "and you know Daddy will *never* accept him!"

I smiled. "I believe he might," I said, "when you tell him he's going to be a *grandpa*."

Julie's eyes went wide. "What? How—how did you know? Did Billy—"

"Nobody told me," I said, "I just read the signs. A woman really *is* more beautiful when she's expecting. Then there's the way Billy is with you—gentle, protective—like you were made of glass. And finally, I caught a look at what Mother Christmas is sewing in yonder. Those are either baby clothes or fixin's for a mighty small grownup."

Well, at that point Julie broke down and fell to crying. I went around to where she sat and held her until she stopped. She came into my arms and kissed me full on the mouth, then stood back at arm's length and watched me blush. "All right. I'll give it a try, cowboy," she said. "Maybe we'll see you one of these days in Dry Creek."

I grinned. "I'll sure be looking forward to that, Mrs. Christmas. Much obliged for the fine dinner—and for your hospitality."

I opened the door, then turned back. My hand found Julie's poetry book in my jacket pocket and I took it out and handed it to her. "By the way," I said, "I reckon this is yours. I found it on a ledge one day over in the Pryor Mountains."

Julie smiled as she took the book from me. Tears welled up in her dark eyes, but I reckon they were happy tears.

Outside, I told Billy he was a lucky man and swung up onto the sorrel. When I topped the first low hill beyond the pasture, I turned to wave goodby. Billy and Julie were standing together arm in arm in front of the house, waving back. He really *was* a lucky man.

The trial of Vince and Ramona Coldwater was held in Silver City the week after I got back from Lander. Ridgeway called on me to testify, and I told the court what I knew about the outlaws' capture, the killing of Cletus Coldwater, and the recovery of some of the stolen money.

It didn't take the jury long to bring in a verdict. Most of the jurors were depositors in the bank, and as far as they were concerned that made the holdup personal. The jury was only out about twenty minutes. When they came back, they pronounced the Coldwaters guilty on all counts, including the killing of the bank teller. The judge sentenced the pair to twenty-five years to life and Vince and Ramona were shipped off to the Territorial Prison at Deer Lodge.

George Keppler, the horse trader and rancher from

Curlew Creek, was convicted of rustling. He was also sent to the territorial pen, but only for five years. I don't believe he would have done any time at all if he hadn't stolen those army mounts. My boss, U.S. Marshal Chance Ridgeway, has little patience for lawbreakers in general, but he gets downright cranky when they violate federal law.

Hoodoo Hawks, my tracker and boon companion, was found innocent of wrong-doing in the shooting of Keppler's man Rafael. I understand Hoodoo's leg wound healed completely, except for a twinge now and then in rainy weather. Lucky for Hoodoo it hardly ever rains where he lives. I heard he's gone back to drinking, but it's not for me to judge him. I reckon everybody needs a hobby. I have no doubt he still charms dogs now and again, but I hope he's gave up dining on horse meat.

As winter settled in, I moved out of the livery barn and took up residence at the widow Blair's boarding house. I still drew my two dollars a day as deputy U.S. marshal, but it was Ridgeway's pleasure that I help Glenn Murdoch out at the city marshal's office. Glenn and me must have been pretty good peace officers. It was so peaceful around Dry Creek during November and the first part of December that it was sometimes hard to keep from falling asleep on the job.

Glenn and me played cribbage a good deal, as usual. One afternoon I actually won a game, but it was only just that once. My cribbage winning streaks tended to be short ones.

We always said nothing changes in Dry Creek, but the week after Thanksgiving Glenn stampeded into the office with news. "You'll never guess what I heard!" he said. "Julie's been found!"

Glenn was so excited he hadn't even bothered to stomp the snow off his feet. I fetched the broom and handed it to him. "You don't say!" I said. "Where?"

"Here in Dry Creek! She came in on the stage this morning and checked in at the Grand Hotel! But that's not all—Julie's married, according to the desk clerk, married to that bronc stomper Thane ran off—Billy Christmas!"

"No!" says I, feeling like a dern hypocrite. "You mean they came here together?"

Glenn said, "That's what the desk clerk says. But they didn't stay in town long—they rented a rig at the livery—said they were going out to the M Cross!"

"Well, I'll be," I said, shuffling the cards. "Some things really do change in Dry Creek."

Just before Christmas, Thane McAllister throwed a big party out at the ranch, and of course I got invited. I thought it was interesting Thane had throwed a Christmas party for a couple whose *name* was Christmas, but it sure was a grand blowout.

Ridgeway was there. Thane, Julie, Billy, and me met with him in Thane's private office and told him the whole story. I expected him to fire me at the very least, or charge me with complicity, malfeasance, or aiding and abetting at the worst. Instead, he just nodded when our tale was told and raised a toast to the happy couple. It wasn't until a week or so later that he called me to account for neglecting to inform him earlier, but even then he was easier on me than I expected.

At the close of the evening we all sang "Silent Night," "O Little Town of Bethlehem," and all them favorite yuletide carols, while Julie played the piano. Later, when most all the guests had gone home, Julie and me sang a chorus or two of "The Gypsy Davy," which might not have been appropriate to the season, but it tickled us no end. There's nothing more fun than a private joke.

I reckon that's pretty much the whole story, except for a mystery that developed during the time Julie and Billy were visiting. Two days after Christmas, some-body caught Waco Calhoun coming out of Jackrabbit Annie's whorehouse and beat him up so bad he wasn't able to work for three months. That same week, two nights later, a person or persons unknown worked Red Murphy over the same way. Neither Waco nor Red could—or would—say who attacked them.

A little mystery keeps life interesting.

Center Point Publishing

600 Brooks Road ● PO Box 1
Thorndike ME 04986-0001 USA

(207) 568-3717

US & Canada:
1 800 929-9108
www.centerpointlargeprint.com